Wicked Angel

(The Wicked Horse Vegas Series)

By
Sawyer Bennett

Find Sawyer on the web!
sawyerbennett.com
www.twitter.com/bennettbooks
www.facebook.com/bennettbooks

Table of Contents

CHAPTER 1

Benjamin

I NEVER UNDERSTOOD online dating. The concept of making a connection through digital written words seems almost impossible.

Not that what I'm doing at this moment is technically dating.

Leaning forward in my chair—a massive executive design made of supple Italian leather—I type a reply to @elencosti89. *Tonight. 11pm. Have a blindfold on. And you should be a little afraid.*

I consider my choice of words before I hit *send*. I've learned enough about this woman to know fear is part of her turn on. I don't know her full name—just her user id of @elencosti89—but I do know her darkest fantasies.

When we connected through the new Wicked Horse Vegas Fantasy app, she admitted her desire to give up absolute control to a stranger. That meant she was going to lay her body out for her partner to use in any way he chose, and she would have no say in it.

She also admitted to being fearful in her submission, and I'm surprised by how much that interests me. I have no clue the reasons behind her wanting to do this, but it's fascinating fear is a motivator for her.

I'm shocked because I can't remember the last time I've been intrigued by a woman.

Even more unusual is the fact we haven't met yet. I've only seen a picture of her, and there's no doubt I'm attracted to the petite woman with chocolate-brown hair and matching eyes. She has no idea what I look like as I didn't bother uploading a photo to the app. I'm not hiding my identity or insecure in my looks. Quite the opposite... I know women find me incredibly attractive.

I just didn't have time. My life is so busy that when the owner, Jerico Jameson, told me about the new fantasy service at the Wicked Horse that matches people by proclivities, I gave it a cursory overview and hastily plugged in the bare necessities of information. I did this after a long day of surgery while I was eating a dried-out bagel with suspect cream cheese from my fridge. Such is the life of a renowned neurosurgeon who concentrates on saving lives and not on proper nutrition.

My app chimes before I can even lay my phone back down on my desk, and I'm surprised when I see a return message from @elencosti89.

Okay, is all she says, and a tiny frisson of excitement travels through me.

I freeze and focus in on the feeling, which is fleeting

and soon sputters out cold. Still, it's something I haven't felt in an exceedingly long time. It's the reason I started going to The Wicked Horse a few months ago—I just wasn't feeling anything. I thought perhaps immersing myself into the seedy depths of kink and dirty sex would spark something, but, so far, my orgasms there have been lukewarm at best. My interest in going has started to wane lately, especially knowing I can do the job with my hand just as well. It's why the fantasy app held some appeal. I thought perhaps I could find something a little more tailor-made for what I needed.

And there it is. I have a fantasy hookup set at the Wicked Horse tonight. I take a moment to reserve one of the new private rooms in The Apartments, which is where Jerico used to live when he first opened the high-end sex club in downtown Vegas, atop The Onyx Casino. It's now an exclusive, super private area the wealthy elite can congregate to live out their dirtiest fantasies if mixing it with the common folks in the other areas of the club aren't of interest. There are three sex rooms within The Apartments that aren't frequently used because they are closed off and secluded, and most people come to the Wicked Horse for the thrill of fucking in front of other people.

I send one more quick text to the private concierge to request rope, soy candles, and an electric vibrator to be stocked inside. That should keep me quite busy with @elencosti89.

There's a sharp knock on my door. Before I can even

grant entrance, it's swinging open. My body tightens when I see my best friend walking through.

Brandon Aimes.

We clicked in medical school, then went into the same specialty of neurosurgery. While he focuses more on spinal surgeries and my love is working on the brain, we both settled in Vegas and founded what has become a much sought-after medical practice because of our skills. Over the years, we have added other doctors, but Brandon and I are the majority owners in Aimes Hewitt Neurosurgical Services, PA.

These days, however, my anxiety flares when I must deal with Brandon. It's obvious by the expression on his face he's not happy to see me either.

He shuts the door, strides to one of the guest chairs on the other side of my desk, then sits with a heavy sigh. I'm not sure if the way he squeezes the bridge of his nose with a brief closing of his eyes is for dramatic flair, but when he opens them, my stomach tightens even further.

"We have a problem," he clips out.

"What's that?" I ask neutrally, not quite sure what I've done now.

"The Harlan family has filed a formal complaint about you to the ethics committee at the hospital." His brown eyes, which are normally warm and friendly, seem to expel frost.

My mind races, trying to remember what, if anything, I did to deserve such a thing. These days, my brain and my mouth aren't often connected in a good way.

Sometimes, I say things I later regret.

"I can see you don't remember, so let me refresh you," he snarls, sitting forward in his seat. "After you scrubbed out of surgery, you met with the wife and two sons, who were obviously upset Mr. Harlan didn't make it. And you told them his brain resembled scrambled eggs and there was only so much you could do to help, but perhaps had he not been drinking and driving, he'd be alive and well today."

Yeah... totally remember saying that. It was the fucking truth, too, but I'm not stupid enough to think that would go without consequences. As doctors who hold human lives within our hands, we have to deal with families using a feather touch.

"Goddamn it, Benjamin," Brandon mutters as he flings himself back into the seat with what seems like resignation. "You have got to get your head out of your ass. You cannot talk to our patients that way. You're going to fucking ruin our medical practice, and I'm about out of patience."

I'd say I'm sorry, but that would be a lie. Peter Harlan was a douche. He'd gotten drunk in a bar, thought he could drive home, then ran off the road and hit a concrete culvert. Without a seat belt on to protect himself, he flew through the windshield and cracked his head open on the drainpipe. His frontal lobe had been scrambled by the time I'd been called in to meet the helicopter that had transported the drunk to the hospital for emergency brain surgery. It was his fucking fault, not mine.

"It's been over a year, Benjamin," he says quietly, but the ice is gone. Now it's just pity and some semblance of understanding. "You have got to move on."

I glance at the clock on my phone. One year, one month, eleven days, six hours, and twenty-three minutes. But who's counting?

He sighs when I refuse to acknowledge anything he's said so far. This isn't the first time we've had this conversation. Anything I might say to defend myself will fall on deaf ears.

Brandon scans my office. It's clean and modern, decorated in black leather and chrome. I'm slightly OCD when it comes to neatness, and everything is pristine.

When he returns his gaze to me, he says, "You made a mistake taking their pictures down."

My entire body jerks as if I'd been zapped by electricity. Although it's been one year, one month, eleven days, six hours, and now twenty-four minutes, Brandon has never once criticized the way in which I've handled the death of my wife and five-year-old daughter.

Until now.

I sense he's reaching his limits of tolerance with the way I'm trying to cope with their deaths. But I'm not sure if he can understand.

More importantly, I don't even want to try to explain it. Like with most things in my life, I only have so much bandwidth available. If I'm to maintain my status as a top-notch surgeon, I have to put my efforts there. Sure, my social skills with patients have taken a nosedive, but at least I'm still fucking amazing at what I do.

If I'm given a brain that hasn't been scrambled, that is.

"Don't you have anything to say?" Brandon demands angrily, noting I haven't said a word since he walked in.

I just stare at him, marveling his ire doesn't even touch me. I don't feel attacked, threatened, or even guilty over his accusations.

Like always lately, I feel nothing.

"You've shut everyone out of your life since the accident," he continues. "Me. Your parents. Your brother. How in the fuck can you live like that?"

While I can technically sit here and listen to him rant for hours, I have some hospital rounds to do. I rise silently from my desk, ignoring the ache in my left thigh, and grab the cane I can't even muster up the strength to loathe, clutching onto the T-shaped handle. My mother bought it for me, and I didn't question its need. My leg still hurts if I put full weight on it for prolonged periods, so I use it all the time.

I remember how hesitant she was to give it to me. She'd had it custom made from ebony wood so I wouldn't have to suffer one of those gaudy aluminum ones with a rubber grip. Not that I'd care.

These days, I don't care about much other than doing my job well. It's all I have the energy to worry about.

I walk around my desk, using the cane to support enough of my weight to keep the pain away. My orthopedic team has assured me it will continue to get better as I strengthen the leg. It's just taking time given the femur was crushed, and I lost a good chunk of my thigh muscle. As it stands, I don't use the cane if I'm walking around a room or a short distance, but it's just easier to take it everywhere with me.

The weight of Brandon's stare presses on me, but like everything else, I just don't care.

"This is serious business with the Harlan family," Brandon says as I move past him. I can hear him lurch out of the chair. His voice follows me out the door, but I don't give him my regard. "You're going to have to appear before the ethics panel."

"Let me know when," I reply, knowing I'm being a dick but not able to help myself.

"Please," Brandon murmurs, and the desperation within that one word almost causes me to stop. Almost.

I leave my office, my limp only slightly pronounced since I've gotten so good at walking with this cane.

"Don't throw everything away," he says, and the warning within is clear. "I can only do so much to help you, Benjamin, but you're making it hard to even fucking do that."

I don't respond as I walk away from him. I'm going to have to pay for my rash words with the Harlans. Deep down, I realize I'm going to have to figure out some way to keep my mouth shut when I get angry at patients.

But that's a worry for another day.

CHAPTER 2

Elena

MY CELL PHONE rings and because my car isn't new enough to rate Bluetooth technology, I have to turn my radio down before tapping on the screen to answer my best friend. The phone sits in one of those contraptions mounted inside my AC vent, and Jorie's face stares merrily out for just a moment before the call connects. I tap again on the screen to engage the speaker phone, all while maneuvering through Vegas traffic.

"What's up?" I chirp, as happy to hear from her today as I was yesterday and will be tomorrow. As best friends, we talk every day.

"The count is up to three hundred and fifty people," she drawls dramatically, and I can envision her eye roll on the other end.

"Wow," I murmur. "That's a heck of a party."

"It's ridiculous," she snaps, and I hold back my snicker of amusement.

"He loves you," I point out. "He's proud of you. He

wants to celebrate the day you were born, and that means your husband is going to go over the top for your birthday. Just sit back and enjoy it."

"I know," she mutters petulantly, but it's obvious she loves how much Walsh loves her. They're childhood friends who fell in love as adults, and I couldn't be happier for them.

Jorie's twenty-fifth birthday is next weekend, and Walsh is throwing a huge party. He wanted it to be a surprise at first, and he'd consulted me about it. I'd said it was a terrible idea because she hates surprises, and he seemed, well... surprised. I had to remind him that yes, he might have been best friends with her brother, Micah, growing up, but he would never know her as well as I do since I've been her best friend since childhood. It was probably an exaggeration, but I am confident she hates surprises.

So he turned it into just a regular birthday party. By regular, I mean it will now include the Vegas elite. It's what happens when your husband owns a successful casino called The Royale, and he's considered Vegas royalty himself.

"So what are you up to tonight?" she asks.

"On my way to The Wicked Horse," I reply, checking my right passenger mirror so I can merge over to the next lane. My exit is coming up soon.

"Oh, can't wait to hear the details," Jorie whispers, and I'm guessing Walsh must be in the room with her. While we share plenty of juicy stuff, she wouldn't breach my privacy to her husband.

Funny how Jorie and Walsh sort of reconnected at The Wicked Horse. They "coincidentally" fucked at a masquerade event, not knowing who the person behind the mask was. Granted, it was an incredibly confusing time between them, especially since Walsh had a tough time accepting his attraction to his best friend's little sister.

But they eventually realized how deeply they loved each other. Now they're happily married, and I take a lot of the credit for it. I was the one who dragged Jorie to The Wicked Horse that night. I wasn't a regular member and couldn't have afforded the yearly membership, but I do treat myself to the exorbitant five-hundred-a-night fee a few times a year. As a woman completely in touch with her sexuality, I find it more than liberating to be able to go somewhere and be surrounded by like-minded people who enjoy celebrating pleasure with one another.

"I'll call you tomorrow," I say as the exit comes into view. "Want to try to get together for lunch soon?"

"I can come your way on Monday," she says. Jorie now lives in Vegas with Walsh in his penthouse suite atop The Royale. I live about half an hour away in Henderson, which is where we all grew up.

"Let's do it," I say without any thought to my calendar. My hair salon is closed on Sundays and Mondays.

"Okay, my love," Jorie says softly and with such affection I'm already looking forward to our call tomorrow. "Have fun tonight."

"Oh, I will," I purr. At least, I think I will. Tonight, I'm trying something different. I'm nervous as hell about it, too.

Normally, The Wicked Horse is about socialization. I go, have drinks, mingle, and meet men. Eventually, I'll meet someone I have a connection with. When I click with someone, we'll hookup. Sometimes, I'll reconnect with a prior lover who I have experience with. Hot, kinky sex follows, and I go home with a smile on my face and the continued freedom from the confines of a committed relationship. It works perfectly.

But I'm going in blind tonight—literally and figuratively. I won't see the man I'll be with. Something about that makes it even more exciting and slightly dangerous. I haven't even met him. We've only exchanged a few messages through the sex club's app. I'm putting all my trust in Jerico Jameson and his assurance he vets his members well.

Because I'll have no say so in what happens to me tonight.

It's my fantasy. As much as the thought of what might happen thrills me, it scares the hell out of me, too.

Which, in turn, thrills me even more.

◆

IN THE LAST message we exchanged today, he'd told me to blindfold myself. Before I did, I read the note the concierge left. When I arrived at The Wicked Horse, an attendant directed me to one of the private rooms in the The Apartments, which is the super exclusive membership within the regular membership. Apparently, my date is affluent because few can afford this level of membership.

The note was simple and not from him, but clearly at his direction.

Please undress fully and put the blindfold on. You're not to remove it at all. You're also not to speak unless you want to use the safe word to stop.

The safe word is crocodile.

Silk sheets in a whitish-silvery color cover the bed in the middle of the room, and they feel cool and soft against my bare skin. The blindfold left for me is extra wide and red silk. I can't see anything, not even a glimmer of light from the edges. Even though I feel a slight panic from not being able to see, I'm completely turned on right now.

Despite the fact the man isn't even in the room with me.

My imagination has been on overdrive all day, but my mind is absolutely spinning with the possibilities right now. He told me there'd be rope, and that I should be a little afraid. I can't help but squirm as I lay back on the cool sheets, trying to regulate my breathing by taking in several slow inhales of air and releasing them just as slowly.

I'm hoping tonight reveals something important about myself. That perhaps I can learn to trust in a man again, even if it's only in bed.

The doorknob rattles slightly, and I go still. My hearing is on high alert, taking over for the loss of sight. Even though the hinges are well oiled, I can hear the whoosh of the door as it opens, and I swear I even feel the flutter of movement it produces along my body. I'd like to say I'm so sensitized it even hardens my nipples, but those tightened up the minute I got naked and put on the blindfold.

The door shuts and I strain to listen, but whoever has walked in—presumably my date—is making barely a sound.

But what if it's not my date?

What if it's some stranger—well, more of a stranger than the man I've been corresponding with—who has stumbled in on me.

I almost reach for the blindfold to take a peek, but I remember the instructions. I'm not to remove it at all. I have to bite my tongue to restrain myself from calling out to whomever is in the room with me.

There's nothing but absolute silence until the soft tap of what must be dress shoes sounds against the hardwood floors, indicating the man—at least, I think I've been corresponding with a man—approaches me.

I mean... what if it's a woman? I hadn't thought

about that. The user ID only said @sinemente1. The profile said "male". At least, I think it did. I don't recall specifically talking about it. What if it's a woman here to do *stuff* to me?

Do I care?

I'm not averse to playing with women in a group, but I'm not inherently attracted to them. Regardless, a man is necessary to fulfill this fantasy. It's all about learning to trust men.

I dig my fingers into the silk sheets, crumpling them in my fist, only to force myself not to remove the blindfold in a panic.

When the mattress dips, I realize whoever it is has taken a seat. It dips quite a bit, indicating someone heavy. So probably a man.

My pulse is galloping, and a sheen of sweat pops out on my forehead.

But then, something warm and large covers my breast. I suck in air and hold it in tight. When I realize a hand covers my entire breast, I know it has to be a man because I'm fairly full-chested. The fingers are long, and I sense strength as well as a delicate touch within.

The hand moves, turns, and then knuckles are running down the middle of my stomach. I continue to hold one large breath inside of me, wondering just how far down he'll go.

When his knuckles graze over my mons, which are waxed bare, my hips rock slightly upward and the air comes rushing out of me.

He doesn't say a word, though.

Doesn't react to my reaction.

Just utter silence before his hand is gone.

The mattress shifts again, and I know he's standing. The tapping of his footsteps resounds as he walks around the bed to the other side.

Then he threads my hand through a rope before something tightens on my wrist. He hoists my arm up and ties it securely to something above my head. It's not painful, but it's not comfortable either.

More tapping against hardwood, then he secures the other wrist.

I wait for my ankles, but they're left alone.

There's a sound I don't recognize at first. A repetitive rasping... once, twice, and then it hits me.

A lighter.

My body tightens, and I strain to hear something else. Anything to give me an idea of where he is now and what he plans to do.

When the first bit of hot wax splashes on my nipple, I hiss in surprise before moaning from the slight sting of pain. It's not bad at all, but then more hits my skin. A flashing burn on my breasts produces a slight sting, then a delicious throb is left in its wake.

I squirm, pull against the rope holding me in place, and start to undulate my hips as more wax drips across the center of my chest to my other breast to burn deliciously over my nipple.

I've never had this done to me before. Never once

considered it. I love to be spanked and spanked hard. Love the combination of pain and pleasure.

And as the stranger pours wax onto my body, I wonder why I never wanted this. It feels incredible. Soon, I can't distinguish between where the pain ends, and the pleasure begins. It swirls together, just as the tiny gasps and moans coming from my mouth do.

The trail of hot wax goes from my breasts down to my stomach. A slow, sweeping pattern left and right, hitting my ribs where I can feel the wax sliding down onto the sheet beneath me.

Lower yet to my belly button. Once again, I suck in a huge breath in anticipation as he gets closer to my pussy. I'm so attuned to what he's doing, and I can tell he's exercising some restraint. There's no longer one long dribble of wax hitting me but instead, I feel individual drops hitting along my bare mons just to the left and right of my slit.

My legs spread, a silent invitation to burn me between my legs. I need it *there*. I think I'll die without it *there*.

No more wax falls, and I cry out in what I think might be actual despair.

"Not there," he says, knowing exactly what I need and denying me. My instinct is to curse at him, but I don't. I remember his instructions. I'm not to speak. He's in charge and it's not about what I want, but about what he chooses to give me.

Right now, I'm completely at his mercy.

CHAPTER 3

Benjamin

I STARE AT the woman—@elencosti89—and, for the first time, I wonder what her name is. Not that I'll ask. I've never asked for a woman's name while at The Wicked Horse because it was irrelevant.

Still is irrelevant. But I do wonder.

She's stunning. I can't see her face because of the wide swath of silk covering it, but I don't need to. I could tell from her picture she was beautiful, but her body is a work of art. It's curved in all the right places, and her skin looks oh so soft. I knew the hot wax would be the right choice.

Those breasts are perfect, her brown nipples begging to be burned.

After she'd taken the first splash like a champ, her entire body had silently begged for more. She squirmed and undulated. Never have I been more pleased to see a woman with a bare pussy, knowing my wax would go there. Only on the outside because I had better plans for her clit than to desensitize it with pain.

When her legs spread, I have to admonish her. "Not there."

Not ever there.

Twisting my body, I set the lit soy candle on the small table beside the bed. I don't extinguish it, but I'm not sure I'll use it again. The candle they gave me is white, and the wax covering her from breast to groin looks like loads of semen splashed all over her body.

I push up from the bed, leaving the woman lying there to wonder what will come next. I've been impressed she's following the rules, which means she's invested in being under my control.

Removing my suit jacket, I head over to the set of built-in cabinets on the far wall. I toss my jacket on a chair in the corner, then loosen my tie. In the cabinet, I pull out the vibrator I'd requested. It's about a foot and a half long with a narrow handle and a bulbous protrusion on the end that vibrates at an impressive speed. To ensure power, it's electric rather than battery operated, and I've seen this tool practically destroy a woman.

In the best possible way, that is.

She's holding perfectly still as I return to the bed. Head raised just slightly and tilted my way as she struggles to listen and perhaps glean what will happen next. I wouldn't tell her even if I could.

But I can't because I have no idea. I'm winging this. Playing it by ear and I'm admittedly slightly off balance.

The fact that my dick is hard as a rock right now is disconcerting. It became that way the minute I let the first splash of wax fall on her breast and she reacted so beautifully. Hating the pain, loving the pleasure, and then, in turn, learning to love and anticipate the pain once again. Yeah, my cock thickened and pressed painfully against my zipper and it's shocking. Despite all the debauchery I've experienced in this place in the last few months since I started attending, my body hasn't quite reacted the way a normal thirty-six-year-old man's body should. It takes a lot to get me going these days, and I don't need my own neurologist, psychiatrist, or any other medical professional to tell me it's all in my head.

Meaning the one that sits above my shoulders.

My dick hasn't worked right since the accident because sex and love were too intertwined for me before. It's abhorrent they should be entwined again.

And yet, here I am in The Wicked Horse, risking that again.

But I have no choice. I have to risk it. Because at least when I'm here, even if it takes me a while to succumb to pleasure, at least I feel something. In the last year of my life, I've gone from suffering unimaginable pain to feeling nothing at all. I was so tired of hurting all the time—of missing my family so badly I'd thought of ending things for good—that I knew I had to do something drastic.

And then one day... I think my psyche just decided

to put up a barrier to emotion. Defensively, it learned the best way to protect myself from the hurt was to ignore it. And I did such an excellent job of it I willed it into non-existence. Along with most every other feeling.

My compassion for my patients seems to have dried up. My camaraderie for my friends is gone. Familial love has gone cold because sometimes I can't even stand to look at my parents and brother. Food tastes bland. The air smells stale. Even my dreams have no meaning and are boring. The only thing that gives me the slightest bit of satisfaction, and it's not even joy anymore like it used to be, is performing a successful operation. But hell... most of what I do in the human brain is rote work. Even that has sort of gone to autopilot and while I feel good if I save a patient, I can't say I feel bad if I lose one.

I'm fucking broken, and I'm trying to get something back. Some sort of feeling.

The last few months have been an interesting experiment. My first few visits here were good, and I thought I'd perhaps found a cure. The orgasms were good, but how could they not be with the level of kink pervading this place?

But then, like with everything else in my life, the goodness faded and the experiences dulled to the point I was about ready to give up my membership.

Until @elencosti89 and I connected on the brand-new fantasy app.

And now my cock is harder than I remember it being

in the last several years, and I bet it gets harder yet once I make her come.

I move to the table by the bed, then squat to plug the vibrator into the electrical socket near the baseboard. I place it on the mattress not far from her shoulder and pick the candle back up again. Concentrating on the smooth, olive toned patches of exposed skin among the framework of cooled wax, I splash more of the fiery substance onto her skin. I peel off the hardened pieces over her nipple before dripping more onto them. My cock pulses in response to her moans of pleasure and the way in which her hips keep thrusting upward. When she spreads her legs wantonly, it tells me it's time to move on.

I get rid of the wax, take the vibrator in hand, and hold it at the ready. Sitting on the mattress at the woman's hip, I press my free hand to the warmth of her pussy. The woman groans, digs her heels into the mattress, and pushes against me. With a short turn of my wrist, I'm able to slip my middle finger into her.

The heat and wetness sucking at my finger causes my balls to tighten painfully and for the first time in forever, I'm looking forward to coming.

I deftly flip the switch on the vibrator and the hum of its powerful little engine whirring causes the woman's head to tilt toward it. She goes still again, despite my finger jammed in deep, then starts to tremble as I move the toy closer.

Ever so slowly, I bring it right to where her clit is hiding under soft bare skin, then press the bulbous, twitching head to her.

I'm stunned when she screams in graphic pleasure, her hips shooting wildly off the bed and she comes harder than I've ever seen before. Faster than I've ever seen. Her muscles contract onto my finger, holding me tight within her, and her entire body shakes with the explosion.

My mouth parts slightly in astonishment at how responsive she is—all from a little hot wax and anticipation.

Once again, her feet dig into the mattress, legs falling open, and she grinds upward into the vibrator as she seeks more.

I press it harder onto her, enough to drive her back down, before I pull my finger out and insert three back in to fuck her with them. She starts a keening whine, wanting to come again and before I know it, she's doing just that.

Another orgasm—not as long lasting but hitting her so hard her toes curl and her arms yank hard at the ropes while her head thrashes.

Spectacularly beautiful.

I flip the vibrator off and toss it carelessly to the floor, not caring if it breaks. I'm done with it for the evening.

Crawling onto the bed, I push her legs farther apart

and settle in between them. I fumble with my pants, eager to get my cock out. It's throbbing, leaking, and so hard I'm almost afraid of what this is going to feel like.

I'm fully clothed, but I don't give a fuck. All I care about is sinking into that slick, dark hole of @elencosti89 and fucking my brains out within her. There's no need for a condom. We both chose to get medical exams so we could have the fully bare experience. Again, I wanted to feel something.

I position the head of my dick to her, putting my hands to the back of her thighs to help raise and spread her legs even more. I glance upward at the woman, able to see just her lips and chin. She's got her perfectly white, straight teeth dug down into her lower lip.

Fuck, that's hot.

There's no entering her gently, but it doesn't matter. She said I could do whatever I wanted to her. Said I could fuck her anywhere and as roughly as I wanted. I have no guilt as I punch my hips forward and slam deep inside.

She finally breaks the rule of no speaking by whispering one word. "Yes."

I can't even admonish her. It feels too fucking good to have her pussy grip me, and my hips start to move.

I know I won't last long, and I don't care if she comes again. She's got two under her belt.

Roaming my gaze all over her wax-covered body, I fuck @elencosti89 and I fuck her hard. Her tits bounce around, and she moans when I hit her deep. She even comes again, catching me by surprise and making my balls pull upward for release.

Ruthlessly, I plunge into her heat and wetness over and over again, not caring if I hurt her, only caring about the storm brewing deep within me. It's like a funnel cloud twirling, tightening, pulling me in.

And then it explodes outward, and I'm coming so hard it hurts.

Hurts beautifully.

My head falls back, and I roar out my release to the ceiling, my hips still slamming into her to draw out every precious drop of feeling I'm unloading into her.

I'm gasping when it's all gone.

In astonishment, I stare at the woman, wondering what in the hell is so special about her since I'm pretty sure that was the best orgasm of my life.

Reaching up with one hand, I pull at the slip knot and release one of her hands.

She immediately brings it to the blindfold, then she starts to push it up.

"Don't," I murmur, locking my fingers around her wrist and pulling it away from her face. "Not until I'm gone."

"I don't care what you look like," she says, and I suppose it's okay for her to break the rules now. We both got what we wanted.

"And I don't care if you care," I say stiffly, pulling

my spent cock out of her and tucking it back into my pants. I roll off the bed and zip up.

Hastily, I go to the chair and snatch my jacket and tie up. Without a backward glance at the woman, I make my way out of the room, a little shaken by the experience.

But also relieved.

Seems I'm not as dead on the inside as I had once thought.

CHAPTER 4

Elena

J ORIE'S BIRTHDAY PARTY is being held in the grand
ballroom at The Royale Casino, which is lavishly
ostentatious in the art-nouveau style. The curved
windows have stained-glass centers, and oriental rugs in
deep reds and navy blues cover the glossy floors. Scrolled
wrought-iron chandeliers hang down the center of the
room, twenty feet apart, and the furniture is heavy with
ornately curved lines and boldly patterned silk cushions.

Once, Jorie confided she hated how opulent it was,
but I suspect that was just a small-town girl trying to
become accustomed to living in her new husband's
wealthy world.

Most people here are Jorie's friends now, too, but
they're mostly from Walsh's world of luxury and wealth.
Prior to reconnecting with her current husband, she had
been living in California coming out of a bad first
marriage. She sort of slunk back into Henderson when
her asshole husband had kicked her out, having the nerve

to tell her she was awful in bed. She showed up on the doorstep to my humble two-bedroom apartment in Henderson, Nevada where we had both been raised, suffering from terrible self-esteem issues because of what that douche had told her. So I promptly made her my permanent roommate and then dragged her to The Wicked Horse to get her back in the saddle—or rather in the bed—and, well... that's the story. She reconnected with Walsh that fateful night, and the rest is history.

And now he showers her with devotion, expensive vacations, jewels, and extravagant parties as is par for the course for a new husband who is crazy about his wife. Not that she wants any of those extravagances. She'd be happy living in a small house in the burbs with her man, but she lets him have his fun.

Well, maybe not a small house. They're trying to get pregnant, and they've been doing so since their honeymoon in Paris last year. They're not going overboard like timing ovulation cycles or anything. I know enough from my bestie that their sex life is robust, and there's a frequent deposit of Walsh's swimmers made in the hopes of getting her pregnant. But past that, they're being laid back about it, figuring it will happen when it happens.

Once, I used to yearn for the same thing, but it's pretty much a non-factor these days. I've had such a string of bad relationships I've given up hope of a good man existing. I mean, sure... there's Walsh, but he's like one in a million. He and Jorie were fated.

I have no one to blame but myself for my bad choices. I pick the same kind of man every damn time. The type who seems confident when things start out, but, before I know it, I've given my heart to someone who is lazy, shiftless, and totally dependent upon me to take care of him both financially and emotionally. I don't know if I have a neon sign flashing above my head or what, but I am the furthest thing from a sugar mama imaginable. I also have no desire to be a grown ass man's mother. Nothing attractive about that.

And it's not like I'm rolling in the money. I'm a struggling business owner and while running my own salon is the height of success for me, it sucks on my soul most of the time with the stress. It's not just about the freedom and the art of styling hair, but about managing employees, rent, bills, supplies, vendors, and customer satisfaction. I work my fingers to the bone, and I don't make much more than I did when I worked in someone else's salon.

Still, there's satisfaction in the accomplishment of keeping the doors open and I don't have to answer to anyone.

At least I have that.

I grab a glass of champagne off a passing tray before walking around the perimeter of the ballroom. I'm here for Jorie, but I don't know anyone other than her brother, Micah. He's currently wrapped up in a discussion with several businessmen and while he'd welcome me into the conversation, it looks like a snooze fest to me.

Jorie's attached to Walsh's hip, where she should be, and he's busy taking her all around the room and showing her off.

As he should.

But she's my bestie and she's worried about me. She glances around frequently to search for me, worried I'm not enjoying myself.

Which I'm not.

Not only do I not know anyone, but I'm also way out of my element. I can guarantee I'm the only hair stylist in this ballroom. Through my hard work and sheer determination, I consider myself middle class, yet I bet I'm the only middle-class person here. This ballroom holds the one-percenters. The people who have six-car garages to hold all their fancy foreign vehicles and jewels on their fingers that cost more than my yearly salary.

But I'm here for Jorie, as I remind myself for the third time tonight. I'll finish this champagne, nosh on some chilled lobster, join in a celebratory piece of cake, and then I'm out of here. Jorie will understand.

"Don't you even think about leaving early," Jorie says as she approaches from behind, grabbing onto my arm. She steers me to the outer edge of the crowd, over to a small nook where there's a stand with a linen-covered tray to collect empty plates and glasses. "I know that expression."

"I don't know anyone here," I whine dramatically. "And you know fancy parties and rich people aren't my thing."

"You screw rich people at The Wicked Horse all the time," she counters with a cocked eyebrow. "So don't even go there."

Which is true, but the only reason I have the luxury is because Jorie bought me a special membership to The Wicked Horse for my birthday last year. It allows me entry twice a month, normally a five-hundred-a-visit value. Prior to my gifted membership, I scraped and scrimped the fee, sometimes giving up a new handbag or pretty dress to get my rocks off a handful of times a year. It was way easier than dating.

Even though she's rich as sin since she married Walsh, I tried to decline the membership because it had to be insanely expensive. But she assured me Jerico Jameson gave her a special deal on the price, and she'd be terribly offended if I didn't take it.

Ultimately, what convinced me to accept her gift were the stars in Jorie's eyes. Given she'd found love in The Wicked Horse, she didn't see why I couldn't do the same. I didn't have the heart to tell her I wasn't interested in it, so I was overly gracious and grateful when I assured her that I loved the gift.

And I did, and still do.

Especially after my encounter last weekend with a faceless man who made my body do things I hadn't known it was capable of doing. How I wish I knew what he looked like. How I wish he would contact me again through the app, because I'd never make the move. To do so would imply I need something from him, and I'm never falling back into that trap again. Yes, my pride is keeping me at bay, but if he did reach out to me, I wouldn't say no to another hookup with him.

I'd jump at the chance.

"You're thinking about him, aren't you?" she asks with a knowing expression. I flush hot—not because she knows me so well, but because the reminder of that amazing evening has me longing for it again.

At lunch Monday, I had filled Jorie in about our time together in the exclusive Apartments. While I didn't give her a play-by-play description, I'd told her enough that she was fanning herself, taking long sips of her iced water, and muttering she and Walsh needed to make a return trip to the club soon.

"I'm not thinking about him," I say out of the side of my mouth, eyes scanning the crowd I'm clearly never going to be a part of. But then I add, "Much."

So many rich people. Beautiful women. Handsome men.

The men here are like everywhere and of no real interest to me. I've found economic status has nothing to do with male character. It might make them appear to have healthier egos, but I've found rich and poor men alike are equally adept at using me.

My gaze moves casually around, admiring the women's dresses more than anything.

"Wow," Jorie murmurs as she sidles in closer to me. "You've got someone's attention."

"Who?" I ask, my head slowly swiveling to take in the people, but then my eyes slam to a stop on a man who is staring with an expression that's difficult to describe. His eyes are hard, almost cold. Jaw locked tight. And yet, he clearly looks surprised to see me, which is weird because he's a stranger to me.

"Do you know him?" Jorie asks, apparently noticing the mixture of emotions that seem to war on his face.

"Not at all. Do you?"

Jorie snorts. "I don't know half the people here. I can go find Walsh and ask."

I turn to face her, mainly to give the man my disregard. I don't know him, he's not important, and I don't feel like fending off someone's advances. Even though he's incredibly gorgeous.

"Oh, man," Jorie whispers as her eyebrows rise high. She gives a nod in the direction of where the man was standing, just over my shoulder. "Here he comes."

My body locks, and I give her an imploring look. "Don't you dare leave me."

"I'm out of here," she says with a devilish grin. "He's totally hot, and he's clearly interested in you."

"No, Jorie," I snap, grabbing onto her wrist. I give her a warning glare. "I'll never forgive you."

"You'll thank me later, I'm sure," she quips before gently pulling herself free from my grasp because I'd never make her stay. It's her birthday after all.

Jorie slips away, and I turn around with a resigned sigh.

I'm shocked as I take in the man walking toward me. As he gets closer, he gets infinitely better looking. Dark hair worn just long enough to be styled in a mussy, just-got-out-of-bed way that's totally hip and fashionable. Sculpted cheekbones, full lips, and a narrow nose that makes him appear aristocratic. He's sporting a very trim, short beard, and his eyes are dark brown and brooding.

What's most shocking is the man is tall, well built, and yet walks with a slight limp while steadying himself on a cane. Intrigue fills me at his youthful age and in-shape physique, the cane only adding a flair of mystery.

When he reaches me, he lets his gaze travel very slowly and almost possessively down my body. It's a move that would normally offend me, yet, somehow, I feel like he has the right to do it.

Weird.

His eyes slide just as slowly upward until they stop and lock on mine.

"You," he murmurs in wonder, and… is that anger?

I blink in confusion. "Me what?"

"I didn't think you could look any better than when you were naked and covered in hot wax, but I'm apparently wrong about that."

A jolt of awareness goes through me as I realize who is standing in front of me, and I feel incredibly off balance. His words on their face would be considered seductive and praiseworthy, but the distinct tone of disapproval in his voice would imply he can't stand the sight of me.

Choosing to focus on his tone instead, I give him a return glare. "Sorry to disappoint."

He seems startled by the vehemence turned on him, taking an unsure step back. He's clearly not an unintelligent man. I can tell by the expression on his face he realizes his mistake right away.

"What I should have said," he says in a gentler tone, "is you look incredibly beautiful tonight. My apologies... I'm not the greatest at giving compliments."

God, he's really kind of weird. His words are right—what any woman would want to hear—but he delivers them so awkwardly it's clear conversing with me is painful. This is so at odds with the confident way in which he handled me at The Wicked Horse last weekend. And there's no doubt this is the man who rocked my world with hot wax, a vibrator, and a very skillful cock. I recognize his voice just from the first two words he had said to me that night.

"Not there."

We stare at each other a moment, and I can see him struggling to try to find something to say. It's not a shyness, but more like an antipathy to carry on small talk. I try to help him out.

"So how do you know Walsh?" I ask.

"Golfing buddy," he replies, then looks around at the crowd. "I normally hate coming to these things, but I promised him I would."

"He wanted to make this a huge celebration for Jorie," I explain before taking a sip of champagne.

"You are friends with her?" he asks as he centers the cane directly before him and rests his hands on top of the ornate T-shaped knob.

"Best friends," I reply with a slight bob of my head. "Grew up together."

He nods and scans the crowd, seemingly at a loss for anything to say. So I ask, "What do you do for a living?"

"I'm a neurosurgeon," he replies as he shifts his attention to me.

I blink in surprise because that's impressive. "Wow."

And maybe that's why he's a little awkward in conversation. Aren't the brilliant types usually that way?

And yet, he doesn't look away again. The expression on his face is contemplative, as if he's trying to figure out the mystery of me. But I'm just me, so it can't be that. I'm pretty much a 'what you see is what you get' person.

He says nothing, and I don't know what else to say either. I'm out of ideas, so I start to figure out how to exit from this conversation, clearly realizing our chemistry revolves solely around sex. Which is fine. We don't need to talk.

"Would you like to go to The Wicked Horse with me?" he asks out of the blue, and I'm taken aback by the almost clinical way in which he states his question. If he were trying to seduce me, he'd do it with softer words or perhaps a caress on my arm.

Instead, it sounds like a boring business transaction.

Still, I want this man again. Never tried to deny that.

Every molecule in my body vibrates, screaming "Yes". I knew I'd jump at the chance to be with him again if the opportunity presented itself, but I find myself regretfully shaking my head. "I can't. My membership only allows me to go twice a month, and I've already used up my allotted days for January. But we could... um... go to your place instead?"

"We can't," he replies flatly, and it arouses my suspicions.

"Why? Are you married?"

"No," he replies staunchly before he grimaces. "It's just that I'm a private person, and I keep sex at the club."

I can understand his reasoning. It's my motto, too, and I want to kick myself for even suggesting going to his place. It seems desperate. Besides, it goes against all the rules I'd put upon myself so I don't fall into a trap again. It's the same exact reason I keep sex strictly limited to the club.

To keep men at arm's length.

Will I never learn?

"But if you'd allow me," he says almost stiffly as if he

doesn't quite trust the words coming out of his mouth. "I'll gladly pay your evening fee to get in tonight."

I locate Jorie standing next to Walsh, and her eyes lock with mine. They're full of questions, but she would never begrudge me if I walked out of here right now on this man's arm.

But with a small sigh of regret, I turn my attention back. "I can't leave until Jorie has her cake."

The man glances over to Jorie and Walsh before bouncing to me. He inclines his head in a way that conveys his disappointment. "Maybe some other time then."

Damn. I had hoped he'd stay for a while until it was appropriate for me to leave, but, clearly, I was just an easy and available conquest in his path. Sounds like he'll head to the club and easily find someone else.

So be it. I don't beg.

"Have a good night," I murmur with a smile, hoping it masks my regret.

After a nod, he heads toward the exit.

I watch him move with an elegant grace despite the slight limp and use of the cane. When he's out of sight, I finish my glass of champagne and take another from a roving waiter.

CHAPTER 5

Benjamin

MY HOUSE IS dark when I walk in. I should do a better job of leaving lights on at night for safety reasons, but it's just not high on my priority list of worries.

I flip on the foyer light, which provides illumination over the spacious living room that leads into the kitchen, then place my cane into an umbrella rack by the door. At one point in my life, it used to just hold umbrellas.

I don't usually bother with my cane in the house. It's not for balance but rather to help take some weight off my recovering leg. I'm able to traverse my house by holding onto walls or counters to help accommodate if necessary.

Moving through the living room, I ignore how ghostly it looks with the furniture shrouded and the built-in shelves empty of knickknacks, mementos, and pictures. When I came home from my lengthy hospital stay following the accident, I had every intention of selling this house. It wasn't my home anymore.

Not without April and Cassidy.

I hired someone to come in and pack away everything. I couldn't bear to look at their smiling faces in the photos April had liberally placed all around our house. Couldn't bring myself to sit on the couch where she would curl up with Cassidy to read her books before bedtime while I would sit in my recliner, perusing some medical journal. I couldn't stand any of it, so I covered it all up and tried to ignore it every time I walked in the door.

My leg is hurting tonight but with no one to see me, I don't try to hide my limp. I hobble into the kitchen, not hungry, but knowing I should eat just for the sake of nutrition. Food tastes bland and lackluster, and I never crave it for enjoyment.

Opening the fridge, I peruse the contents. Mustard, mayonnaise, ketchup in the door along with some pickles. Leftover containers of Chinese food that are probably over a week old. A few protein drinks and some moldy bacon.

Closing the refrigerator, I pull open the freezer drawer underneath. A handful of frozen dinners that don't entice.

Back into the fridge I go, snagging two protein shakes. I uncap them both and as I stand with one hand resting on the granite countertop of the kitchen island, I drink them one right after another. Guzzling without tasting because I couldn't even if I tried. I toss the empty containers in the trash, then move through the shadowed house.

I don't bother looking into Cassidy's room. The door has remained closed since I returned home from the hospital, and I don't have the guts to even peek inside. I ignore the double doors at the end of the hall that provide entrance into the master suite.

If I were to go in there, like everywhere else, drop cloths would cover the furniture. I even had them remove the mattress because it smelled like April, and I didn't want the reminder should I have to go in there for some reason.

Instead, I head into the guest room I'd taken over. The furniture and decor in here had not meant anything to me. There wasn't even one family photo in here to be dealt with. Just a comfy bed with a neutral-colored comforter. It's where my parents stayed when they came to visit from Michigan or where April's twin sister, Angela, slept when she passed through Vegas on occasion. I'd added a small desk near the window that overlooks the front yard, then equipped it with a laptop I can do work on late at night. I don't sleep as much as I used to so my paperwork has never looked better.

Flipping on the bedside lamp, I let myself sink into a sitting position on the edge of the bed. The immediate relief to my leg causes an involuntary sigh to escape, and I rub my hand across my beard.

This is my home life existence. A ten-by-twelve guest bedroom and an empty fridge.

And yet, I don't feel like I'm missing out on anything. Living has become quite simple for me. I keep my attachments to people and luxuries to a minimum, concentrate on my job, and put all my energies into saving lives. I don't worry about anything else. By not giving anything value, nothing can hurt me if taken away.

Self-preservation at its finest.

And yet, I'm in a conundrum because I've just recently found something that has proven valuable to me.

At least on one occasion.

The woman from The Wicked Horse Vegas last weekend. If I were being honest in the brutal, flagellating way I've developed over the last year, I'd call her a plague because she's occupied way too many of my thoughts since our encounter. It's disconcerting because the only thing I've allowed to penetrate any of my brain matter, is well… brains.

Those I operate on, evaluate, and fix. I only have room for work, or so I thought.

But this past week, I repeatedly replayed every single moment of that evening over in my mind. I wasn't with her more than thirty minutes tops, yet I've spent hours analyzing every minute of it. Why this woman fascinates me is vexing, because on the surface, she's no different than any other beautiful, hot, fuckable woman at the club.

I'm not sure how many times I went into the fantasy app since our hookup, intent on setting another meeting.

Another chance for me to feel something.

And while she might be labeled a frustrating annoyance to me in so many ways, I must admit she has proven to have value to me.

Because my body reacted differently to her than any other of my conquests in The Wicked Horse. For the few months I've been a member, I've fucked my fair share of the women there and I've gotten off each time. But I'm not sure it's been worth the exorbitant fee I pay to be a member.

At least not until last Friday night with the mysterious @elencosti89 and what was the most mind-blowing sexual experience of my life. It all boiled down to the fucking orgasm that made me almost believe in God again.

Yes, she has value. She made me feel again, and isn't that the reason I went to The Wicked Horse in the first place? Because I'd gotten so far removed from life itself that I wasn't feeling much of anything. Even I know it's not a good thing, and it is only a thin line separating what I had and the peace that might come with death if I thought about things too hard.

So why in the hell had I passed up the opportunity to be with her again? My entire body pulsed with energy when I saw her standing in that ballroom. A blindfold hid most of her face, but I'd seen her picture before. She was easy to recognize because she's such a beautiful woman.

It was a simple proposition. I could have brought her to the club after they'd served the cake at the party tonight, but I shut that down. Having another divine sexual experience was within my grasp, but I turned my back on it.

Same old Benjamin. Shielding himself. Taking the easy way out. Being a coward.

I could have fucking had her tonight, and I passed.

Because despite how desperately I've been seeking to feel something the last few months, it scared the shit out of me once it happened.

It means I'm not totally dead inside.

And that means I can hurt again.

"Goddamn it," I mutter as I scrub my hands through my hair. No good choices.

April would be shaking me right about now if she were corporeal. I imagine her as a spirit somewhere but not in Heaven. I can't believe in such a place because I can't believe in a God who would do such an awful thing to our family.

I can almost understand April. She had not lived a complete life, but a full one. But what the fuck had Cassidy ever done to ever deserve to die that way? Why would God do that to a five-year-old?

Again, I can almost envision April shaking her head

sadly at me for thinking these thoughts. She'd wonder where her eternal optimist had gone.

It's easy for me to ignore these thoughts as April's face dulls and fades more each day. Without the pictures out to remind me of how beautiful and sunny she was, I sometimes struggle to remember what she looked like. The memory of Cassidy's face faded a bit faster, since I'd had less time with that precious angel.

And then something uniquely horrific hits me straight in the middle of my chest. A pain so intense that nausea sweeps through me. Groaning as I rub my breastbone, I try to put meaning onto what I'm feeling.

Guilt.

Pure, exquisitely sharp and brutally unforgiving.

Tears prick at my eyes for the first time in months. Not since my mom told me April and Cassidy had died in the accident.

They had put me in a medically induced coma so I could cope with my multiple injuries. They'd brought me out of it eight days later and my mom's face was the first thing I saw as my eyes fluttered open. My mouth was dry, and I tried to talk but couldn't.

"You have a trach," were the first words out of her mouth as she leaned over the bed to hover in my field of vision. I could tell by the expression on her face she was holding onto some horrible, awful secret. "Don't try to talk."

My gaze moved left and right and there were two

nurses checking me out. I hurt all over, but that's not what caused me to want to slip back into unconsciousness.

It was the sickening expression on my mom's face.

She grabbed my hand, gently of course, and leaned in even closer. "You're going to be all right. You've been in a medically induced coma for eight days to help you cope with your injuries."

It was impossible to talk, but I spoke with my eyes. I stared at my mom, imploring silently for her to tell me everything. Because I remembered April in the front passenger seat and Cassidy in her child safety seat in the rear when a pair of headlights crossed over into our lane of travel and came barreling at us.

My mom's eyes filled with tears, and she gave a sad shake of her head. "I'm sorry, Benjamin. I'm so sorry. But April and Cassidy didn't make it."

I'm not sure if I'd been crying or not. I'd felt such painful emotion deep in my lower throat, but it couldn't rise any higher than the trach. My eyes blurred, and warmth hit my cheeks. Pain spread through my chest, so severe I thought perhaps the stress of this news was killing me. It moved down into my stomach, and it seemed to curdle there.

My mouth opened and I gasped like a dying fish, but no sound came out.

I'd cried in the only way my broken body would let me, and it hurt so fucking much to do it so quietly. All the pain and grief stayed pushed down deep. By the time my trach was removed and I was released from the hospital almost three weeks later, I'd learned to keep it pushed down.

I haven't shed a tear since.

The guilt within me continues to pulse, and I breathe through the pain.

This is a good thing, I remind myself.

It means I'm feeling something.

And the only thing I can give credence to for this breakthrough is @elencosti89.

I don't even know her name, but I know she's broken something open.

I lean on my hip, pulling my cell out of my pocket. Within moments, I have the fantasy app open and I'm sending her a message before I can talk myself out of it.

I'm disappointed not to spend time with you tonight. Let's meet again, at your convenience. I'll gladly pay your entrance fee into the club for the pleasure of your company.

Setting the phone on the bedside table, I wonder if she's still at her friend's birthday party or if she's made her way home yet. I wonder where she lives and what she does for a living. I never even thought to ask, even though the polite thing would have been to engage in conversation after she'd asked what I did.

Pushing up from the bed, I suppress the groan that wants to bubble out from the pain in my leg. It would be so easy to succumb to narcotic pain meds to help ease the burden. Instead, I'm using old-fashioned perseverance in my therapy and workout regimens, the dull support of a cane, and a gratefulness the ache in my leg takes my mind off other things.

I limp over to the guest bathroom, then strip out of my clothes. It takes me no more than five minutes to take a hot shower and brush my teeth.

When I make my way back into the guest room where I sleep, the phone draws my gaze. I can see there's a notification on the icon of the fantasy app.

I plop down on the edge of the bed, the damp towel I'd wrapped around my waist gaping and exposing the fourteen-inch scar running along my outer left thigh. The scar itself looks like someone gouged out a chunk of muscle in the shape of a thin triangle about three inches in width at the widest point. My hand rubs at the scar, feeling the hardware underneath the reddened, puckered skin where I have plates and screws holding my femur together.

My other hand shakes slightly as I pick up my phone, then use my thumb to tap on the app. I maneuver to the messaging system, and my heart lurches when I see the response is from @elencosti89.

Tomorrow night? 11pm?

The weird sensation of my lips curving upward startles me a moment, but then I'm typing back.

Perfect. Meet you in the lobby.

CHAPTER 6

Elena

I N ALL THE times I have been to The Wicked Horse, I have never met someone in the first-floor lobby. Even though an evening at the club pretty much guarantees a fuck, there's still work to be put in to meet and match up with someone who can fulfill the desired fantasies. That means socializing and talking beforehand.

Tonight, it's not necessary, which makes it feel a little bit like an arranged date. I hate to think of it that way since nothing about tonight resembles a traditional date. We're certainly not going to be having extended conversation while trying to get to know each other. Let's face it... we know all we need to at this point.

We are well matched in our sexual chemistry and needs.

The Wicked Horse sits on the forty-sixth floor of the Onyx Casino in downtown Vegas. There is a private elevator that runs from the first-floor lobby straight up to the sex club and I stand near it waiting for my "date" to arrive.

So weird to even think of him as a date. I don't even know his name. Only that he's a neurosurgeon. I suppose I could address him as "doctor," but that seems weird.

Admittedly, I am beyond excited and nervous at the same time. I honestly did not think I would hear from the man again. There was something about the way he'd left Jorie's party last night that clearly stated he wasn't interested. Sure, he tried to hook up with me, but because it wasn't on his exact terms, he'd moved on. I'd been disappointed, but I didn't think he felt much of anything about our ships passing in the night.

I glance at my watch, my entire body buzzing with anticipation. It almost feels like I've been roofied. Not that I would know what it felt like, but I can suspect since I feel overly primed to have this man fuck me again.

Inside my small purse, my phone chimes with a text. The handbag is a simple black silk number that matches the black dress I'm wearing. It's sexy but also elegant, which is the expected dress code for The Wicked Horse.

I reach in and nab my phone, flipping to the text screen to see what Jorie wrote.

I am officially three days late on my period.

I put my purse under my arm to hold it tucked against my ribs, which frees my hands so I can respond. *What? Are you serious?*

I hit send, waiting only a moment before she replies.

Yes!!!

I go dizzy with giddiness that Jorie might be pregnant. I'm not surprised she would share this with me, even though three days late doesn't prove anything. But we have the deep, abiding bond of trust between us. Being besties will never change, which means we share even the tiniest of thrills, hopes, and expectations.

Which causes a twinge of guilt I'm getting ready to meet the mysterious man from her party last night, and I haven't even told her about it. For some reason, I want to keep this experience to myself, at least for tonight. And it's because he is so different from any other man I have been with. In fact, I'm walking into this evening fully expecting it might not end up as great as last time. If that ends up the case, I'm going to be disappointed. But I'm not ready to share the possible let down with Jorie, so I haven't mentioned anything. I don't want her to get all hopeful I might find something special the way she did.

Before I can respond, Jorie texts again. *I've got to go. Walsh and I are headed out to the drugstore for a pregnancy test and some late-night ice cream. Love you.*

I sent her a quick text back. *Love you, too. Good luck. Let me know results asap.*

She blows me a kiss with an emoji, and I smile.

As I turn off my phone, a pair of black dress shoes come into my line of vision. I slowly lift my head. Standing before me is my date, and he looks even better than I remembered.

He's wearing a light gray designer suit complete with matching vest and accessorized with a white dress shirt and pale pink tie. Like last night, his hair is slightly mussed, yet his beard is perfectly trimmed. I wonder what it would feel like between my legs?

He lets his dark eyes run down my body, and I feel a moment of triumph when I see them heat up. When his eyes lock onto mine, he remains stoically silent. It's awkward because I would usually expect a compliment over how I look at this point.

My heart sinks a moment, wondering if he is going to be awkward or shy, a complete juxtaposition to his commanding ways our first time together. I absolutely don't want to have to lead. It's why the fantasy app had matched us to begin with—I want someone I can submit to who will have absolute control over me. I don't want to have to be the idea person, the seductress, the vixen who will rock his world.

I mean… I want to rock his world, but I want him to rock mine in return. That's what he did for me the other night.

I want it again.

I'm startled when he grabs my hand, then turns me toward the elevator. "I've been thinking all day about what I want to do to you."

His voice is deep, dark, and rumbling with pent-up desire. A pleasurable cramp hits me straight between my legs. Instantly, I feel a rush of wetness just from those words. It's not a compliment about how I look tonight, but rather how I've affected him since our first encounter, which is much better.

I don't respond because I don't feel there's any need. Instead, I intend to follow and comply obediently with whatever he wants to do.

I follow him into the elevator and when we emerge at the hostess podium, he gives a curt nod to the woman before he leads me through The Social Room. It's where I'd ordinarily start my evening by having a drink or two to relax and meet prospects.

I'm led into another small lobby that has several hallways leading from it. Turning to the right, he heads straight for The Apartments.

This surprises me. I thought he might want to exercise control over me in a more public way. I had envisioned him putting me in the stocks or maybe on a St. Andrew's cross in The Silo. The glassed-in rooms are the perfect place to exhibit kink for everyone to see.

Once inside The Apartments, he leads me to the same private room we were in last week. Except when he opens the door, I'm stunned to find it looks completely different. The bed, which I'd laid on as I'd allowed him to pour hot wax over me, is gone, and instead, there's a black leather harness suspended from the ceiling. There are so many straps I can't even comprehend how it works. Beside it, there's a thick cable that appears to hold a remote control to maneuver the contraption.

I can feel my nipples go tight against the material of my dress as this is something new. I've never been suspended in any kind of contraption, and I'm going to be helpless as I hang there. Glancing around the room, I see a rolling metal cabinet with three drawers. Past that, there's nothing else to see.

He drops my hand, then moves to the cabinet. Opening the top drawer, he withdraws the same red silk blindfold I'd had on the night before.

Turning, he holds it out to me. "Get naked and put this on."

There is no doubt I will do exactly as he says. I saunter up, then take the blindfold from him. He watches me with heavy-lidded eyes as I shimmy out of my dress. His nostrils flare when he sees I'm not wearing anything under it.

"Leave the shoes on," he commands.

I push the stretchy material of my dress down past my hips along my legs, then step out of it without managing to wobble once in my extremely high heels.

To my surprise, he moves toward me, taking the blindfold out of my hands.

"Turn around," he orders gruffly.

I comply, feeling him step in close, then I'm plunged into darkness as he ties the red silk around my eyes.

I gasp when he reaches around and pinches my nipple lightly, causing my hips to fly back into him. Blind, I can only imagine what is going to happen. I'm not prepared when one strong hand goes to my hip and the other brings his cane around to where he gently rubs it across my naked pussy. Moaning, I try to press into him, but then he's gone and I'm all alone in the dark.

I stand there, wobbly and uncertain, listening intently for anything to give me a hint as to what he'll do next. Part of the excitement is not knowing. For all I know, there's a flogger in that cabinet that he could use to redden my skin soon.

But all I hear is a click, then some whirring. Footsteps pad toward me, then his hands are on my shoulders guiding me forward a few steps until he halts my progress.

With a series of soft commands, he starts to put me into the contraption.

"Raise your right leg."

"Lift your arms."

"Squat down just a tiny bit so I can get this strap on."

Every single maneuver binds me tighter into the contraption. I feel swaths of leather crisscrossing all over my body. Several down my legs, under my ass, across my back.

Snaps click into place, and the swish of leather into buckles sounds. I also hear *him*.

His heavy breathing gets more labored as he binds me into the harness. What I wouldn't give right now to feel how hard he is…

"There," he murmurs, and it's a word of completion filled with satisfaction. There's admiration in his tone for how I must look right now.

Helpless and at his mercy.

I can hear him—no, feel him—as he steps in closer to me, and I'm stunned when his lips brush softly across mine. For some reason, I didn't think kissing would be part of our rendezvous tonight, but just as quickly, he's gone once again. A waft of air floats across my body as he steps away, and I strain to listen.

There's a click, then I'm being hoisted ever so slowly into the air. I go to my tiptoes, but then my feet are off the ground. Strips of leather support me under my ass as well as across my upper back, keeping me from flipping upside down. He'd secured my hands together at the wrist, then locked them onto what feels like a bar above my head.

Another click and a whirring of gears, and I'm stunned as the numerous straps tied from my upper thighs down to my ankles start to pull my legs apart obscenely.

I go up, up, up and still… the movements pull my legs farther apart, stretching them to capacity.

Another click and I stop, swaying gently back and forth.

I'm surprisingly comfortable except for the fact he's splayed me open. I can't stop the flush of embarrassment heating my cheeks.

In the utter silence, I start to quiver in a mixture of fear and anticipation. Is pain coming? Pleasure?

Nothing prepares me for the utter warmth that covers my pussy. It takes me a moment to realize his mouth is on me, his intent to destroy me orally. I have no clue how high I am, nor how his body is positioned, but he seems to be in absolute control as he holds nothing back.

His arms come underneath me, grabbing onto the straps just under my butt to prevent the harness from swaying. Holding me in place and using the leverage of my immobility, he plunges his tongue deep inside of me. He groans—either in satisfaction over the way I taste, that I'm completely helpless and at his mercy, or both.

The pleasure is so intense I start gasping and moaning. He licks and fucks me with his tongue. His teeth bite gently before he sucks hard on my clit. He is relentless in this pleasurable torture, and I come exquisitely hard after only a few moments, the force of the orgasm tearing through me and causing me to shriek.

He doesn't stop, though. Just voraciously attacks me with his mouth again. He brings a hand to my pussy, plunging his fingers in. One, two, and sometimes even three. I am so wet, and he's drawing reactions from my body I've never given to anyone else.

A finger slides across sensitive skin to my ass before probing gently. Just as he lashes at my clit with his powerful tongue, he presses his long finger into my most forbidden place.

As I wail from the sensations, another orgasm hits me hard as he continues to eat me. Powerful ripples of ecstasy rocket through my body, making me delirious.

Tears slip from the corners of my eyes, running along my temples, and I imagine them splashing to the floor.

Damn that feels so good. I want to stay lost in this moment forever.

It barely penetrates but what sounds like a remote control clicks, then I can feel the contraption lowering me. As I drop downward, his mouth stays locked onto my wet flesh and he continues to pleasure my over-sensitized flesh with his tongue.

Another click.

His mouth is gone, and he rotates me. Flips me. My stomach rolls slightly even though the machine moves at a snail's pace. I think I might be facing the floor now, but I'm not sure.

After another click, the straps start tightening to draw my legs slightly inward again.

I'm startled when I feel my knees press into the cool tile floor, then my torso with my arms stretched out in front of me. I turn my face, pressing my cheek onto the smooth floor.

The harness stops moving and before I know it, I can feel him kneeling at my backside as he uses his hands to push my legs slightly apart. He tips my ass into the air, then his hands are on my buttocks.

I groan when I feel the fat head of his cock pressing into my pussy. He grips me by the hips hard as he plunges in so deeply it makes me cry out.

It could be minutes or hours. All I know is he relentlessly pummels me from behind, and it's the best thing I have ever felt in my life. Bound in leather, held helplessly to the floor, and impaled on this mysterious man's erection, I know there is something special between us.

A third orgasm starts brewing deep inside, and the man sounds like an animal with his grunts and groans as he fucks me so hard my teeth are rattling.

I explode once again in pleasure, feeling my inner muscles locking tight and he feels it, too.

"Fuck, yeah," he growls in praise as he plants himself deep inside of me.

Like he did the first night, he roars out his satisfaction as he unloads inside of me, his fingers digging so deep into my ass muscles there will be bruises tomorrow. Something about his release is so animalistic it connects to something deep inside I've never shared before.

I want to bring out the animal in this man. Revel in it.

He collapses onto me, his torso pressing into my back. At this point, I realize he's still fully clothed as his hips continue to rock into me while he pants slightly from the exertion.

I feel him shift, then his lips are at my jaw. He doesn't kiss me, but I can feel his whiskers rubbing against my skin in an almost affectionate way.

"I have a proposition for you," he murmurs through the haze of waning lust.

I'm still panting, feeling the remaining tremors of my own orgasm pulse through me. "What's that?"

"Let me buy you a thirty-day membership here," he says, and I cannot deny the pull of the seductiveness in his tone. "Give me exclusivity for thirty days. Be at my beck and call whenever I want."

And that's it. His offer. Fuck him exclusively for thirty days here at The Wicked Horse. Whenever he wants.

I don't need to think about it. Sure, it will be hard since I work long hours and live in Henderson, but it doesn't matter. "Okay," I quickly reply before he can change his mind.

"Okay." He exhales on what sounds to be a relieved sigh, and it makes me smile.

"I'm Elena by the way," I say.

"Benjamin," he murmurs.

CHAPTER 7

Benjamin

I WALK OUT of the surgical room, peeling off my gloves with a snap before I toss them in the medical refuse bin followed by my scrub cap. I give a quick wash to my hands, tossing my head left and then right to pop the bones in my cervical spine. Normally a twelve-hour surgery to remove an acoustic neuroma would leave me exhausted, but while my body is feeling a slight fatigue, I'm feeling strangely fresh and rejuvenated.

It has nothing to do with the surgery I just successfully performed, but rather the fact I'm meeting Elena in approximately three hours at The Wicked Horse.

It's been five days since I last saw her and my need for her has grown exponentially as each day has passed. When I made my offer of the thirty-day club membership and exclusivity between us, I had imagined having her every single night. This week turned into a cluster fuck between our two schedules. Both of us work long days, which extend into early evenings. One night, Elena had a family function she had to attend. Two nights, I had to fill in for Brandon on call as he was sick. Another night, Elena had a flat tire and it was too far to drive into Vegas from Henderson on the spare.

I'm exhausted right now, and I know she wouldn't hold it against me if I canceled. But my need for her has grown to an almost painful one, and I don't care if I have to crawl to the club... I'm going to have her tonight to make up for the days we missed—more than once I'm sure.

"Great job in there," Melissa Corbin says as she comes out of the operating room. She was the anesthetist for my surgery today.

Lifting my chin in acknowledgment, I give her a short smile. Her eyebrows raise in surprise at the sight. I haven't bestowed many smiles over the past year, and it bothers me that it shocks her.

Turning to my left, I toss the used paper towels in the garbage and head out of the scrub room, nabbing my cane, which I'd left by the door since I don't need it in the surgical room with me. Sometimes, I perform standing, other times sitting on a stool, but always with the ability to lean against something.

I barely make it through the scrub room door before I come up short, face to face with my partner Brandon. His face is grim. "We need to talk."

"About what?" I ask defensively, because let's face it... lately any time Brandon has tried to talk to me, it's been because I've fucked up.

"Peter Harlan's family has sued you and the medical practice, which includes me."

"Fuck," I mutter, scrubbing my beard with worry.

"Let's go to my office," Brandon suggests, and I have no choice but to follow him. Medical malpractice isn't a discussion to have in the open hallways.

We maneuver through the hospital, then into an underground tunnel that leads to an office building next door. It houses several medical practices, but I head to the fourth floor where our neurosurgery offices are located. The entire journey, which takes almost five minutes, is completed in silence. I don't use the time to figure out how to defend myself, but rather think about Elena and how I'll get to forget about this when I'm inside of her later tonight.

Images of her in that harness flash before me. My mouth waters as I remember her taste. My groin tightens as I remember the soft feel of her around me, and I experience an almost unmitigated sense of jubilation over seeing her tonight by the time we make it to Brandon's office.

He motions to the guest chairs and I take one, putting my cane across my thighs. Brandon doesn't move behind his desk. He just leans against it with his arms crossed.

"I didn't do anything wrong during that surgery," I say adamantly, because it's obvious he wants me to defend my actions. "You saw the records. The test results. That man's brain was beyond saving, and I'm not going to pay for something that wasn't my fault."

Brandon bends forward slightly to bring his face a bit closer to mine. "It is your fault, Benjamin. You treated that family poorly, and it pissed them off. That's why they sued. It's your fault we're in this predicament, no matter how the surgery turned out."

His defense of them infuriates me. He's not taking my side as a partner and best friend should, which pisses me off even more.

I rise from my chair, lowering the end of the cane to the floor to lean against it. "No, they sued us because they feel guilty they couldn't control that drunk son of a bitch. They knew what he was. Sat by while he got DWI after DWI. They enabled him. It's as much his family's fault as anyone's."

The anger leaves Brandon's face, and he gives a long sigh of resignation. "You don't know that," he murmurs.

"Don't I? You should know just how true that can be."

Brandon shakes his head. "Not everyone is like Marcus Pettigrew. You've got to learn to put that aside. Stop judging everyone—"

"Or what?" I demand.

Brandon stands up, his height equal to mine and we are now eye to eye. "Or we can't practice together anymore. You're putting my family and me at risk,

Benjamin. And I just can't allow that."

His words hit me hard. Right in the center of my chest, which constricts in guilt. It's the same exact feeling I had when I'd learned April and Cassidy died in the automobile accident. I had such tremendous guilt I had lived, and they hadn't. And here I am, putting everything important to Brandon at risk.

And, in a way, he's right. I tend to judge everything based on my experiences since that drunk driver, Marcus Pettigrew, crossed the centerline and hit our vehicle head-on.

Taking everything good and beautiful and important to me away in an instant.

Now, every drunk is the same as him. Every person with flaws isn't worthy of my skills. I have no leniency, and I judge harshly.

It's all coming down on me now, though.

"I'm sorry," I say softly... genuinely. "You don't deserve any of this."

Brandon blinks in surprise, his mouth falling open. "You never apologize for anything. At least, not since the accident."

This is true. I've pretty much been a withdrawn asshole to my friends and family since the accident. I give a slight shrug. "Well, I *am* sorry for causing you problems. I'll handle this with the ethics board. You have my word. And you know my work on that man was solid, and there was nothing I could do to save him. You know it, Brandon. But I promise I'll make amends. I'll even apologize to the family for my behavior. This lawsuit won't go anywhere."

My friend—former best friend, perhaps, since I haven't been particularly good to him lately—raises a skeptical brow. "Who are you and what have you done with Benjamin?"

My smile is thin. I know he's trying to get me to show some spark of positive emotion, but some of my pain is too thick to penetrate all the way. All I can offer him is, "You know I don't do anything to intentionally hurt anyone."

Brandon sighs and nods. "I know. Doesn't mean you haven't hurt people all the same."

There is no arguing with that. I've pretty much alienated Brandon—my parents and my brother, too. They are the closest people to me in this world. In my fucked-up mind, I won't suffer when I eventually lose them if I can manage to keep them at arm's length. They are smart enough to realize that's why I've withdrawn. Even though they've been respectful of my needs and given me the space I've demanded over the past year, they've suffered over it, too.

With a slight cough, Brandon gives me a resolute expression. "I'd like to go over the lawsuit tonight so we can meet with our attorneys tomorrow. Come up with a game plan. Let's go grab a late dinner to discuss it."

Overwhelming disappointment floods me. The asshole in me—the one who has become quite dismissive of everyone's feelings except my own over the past year—wants to tell him to go to hell. I've got a hot date with a siren at a sex club. But I'm also warring with the guilt over the trouble my rash actions have caused Brandon.

Rubbing at the nape of my neck in frustration, I finally nod. "Let me grab my things from my office, then I'll meet you in the parking garage."

Brandon lifts his chin in acknowledgment before turning to gather files from his desk.

I move toward the door, but he stops me. "Hey, Benjamin?"

Planting my cane into the floor for balance, I twist to look at him.

"Don't forget the charity benefit for the children's hospital tomorrow night," he says pointedly. "Dr. Metzer is chairing it."

Dr. Metzer.

Head of the ethics committee. The man who will determine my fate over the way I dealt with the Harlan family.

Damn it.

"It would be a tremendous help if you went," Brandon reasons. "Act sociable. And sane. Show him you were just having a bad moment instead of a bad year."

A low growl of annoyance and frustration leaves me, particularly because he's right. And I owe him.

"Okay. I'll go."

"Good man," Brandon says with a grin.

I head to my office, which is just two doors down from Brandon's. I grab my backpack, which I use to carry my laptop and other electronics. Fishing my cell phone out, I pull up The Wicked Horse fantasy app.

Regretfully, I type out a message to Elena.

I'm sorry, but I need to cancel tonight for work reasons.

After I hit send, another idea occurs to me.

But would you be interested in attending a charity gala with me tomorrow night?

She would at least make the evening more enjoyable. While I'm not keen on conversation these days, I'm genuinely curious about her.

Afterward, we could make the night worth it by hitting the club.

CHAPTER 8

Elena

"THAT DRESS LOOKS fabulous on you," Jorie exclaims as she claps her hands.

Examining myself in the full-length mirror in Jorie's master bathroom, I have to agree. I look stunning. It's an off-the-shoulder, A-line cocktail dress in a pinkish-gold with a paint-splatter design in black along the hem. Far more elegant than anything I have ever owned or could afford. Luckily, my bestie is married to a man who needs a fashionably attired woman on his arm, so her wardrobe is brimming with beautiful dresses, and oh... we wear the same size.

When I told Jorie I'd been invited to a charity gala "by a man I'd met online" and needed her help, she was beyond excited. She is so brimming with happiness over her own newfound love she wants the same for me. Wants me to find my own personal happiness, get married, and have babies we can raise together. Any time there's a whiff I might have a date or an interest in a man, she gets over-excited.

Which is why I still haven't told her about Benjamin, which is obviously weighing heavily on my conscience. More so because Jorie is indeed pregnant. After letting her husband in on the secret, I was the one and only other person she shared the information with. She had told me there was no way she was going to wait until the end of her first trimester like many people do before letting her best friend in on the singularly most happy event of her life.

And yet, I still can't bring myself to tell her about the mysterious man who I have had two mind-blowing, carnal experiences with. Part of me is afraid I am going to jinx it with him if I let anyone in on this. I simply can't let myself give credence to something so power-ful—that could potentially have the power to change me in a fundamental way. Until I can get a handle on exactly what this is, I have resolved to tread carefully and quietly.

I let Jorie put some finishing touches on my makeup while she chatters on about being pregnant. She has an appointment with her obstetrician next week for a formal pregnancy test, so she can get started on her prenatal care.

When she finishes my makeup, fluffs my hair once more, and pronounces me sufficiently beautiful, we leave the master suite to find Walsh waiting in the living room.

Offering his arm to me, he says in an over-exaggerated British accent, "Let me escort you down-stairs, milady."

Rolling my eyes, I laugh, but loop my arm through his all the same. Jorie links arms with me on the other side, and we make our way down the private elevator, through the lobby, and out the doors to the Vegas strip.

Walsh keeps walking, though, and heads straight toward a black limo parked in front.

I stop dead in my tracks as I stare at the limo driver who opens the door.

"What is this?" I ask.

"I'm giving you my limo for the evening," Walsh says. "So get in the damn chariot."

"But it's only a few blocks down to The Presario," I say, trying to protest his generosity.

Jorie steps in front of me, then gives me a hard hug. "Get in the damn limo. Walsh is feeling overly generous because he's so happy to become a daddy."

I pull away from Jorie and turn to Walsh, going on to my tiptoes to give him a kiss on his cheek. "You're a prince. Thank you."

"Don't I know it," he replies with a wink before helping me into the car.

It only takes a few moments to drive the two blocks down the strip to The Presario, one of the newer casinos, where the gala is being held. I see Benjamin waiting for me in front. He looks amazing in a tuxedo, his cane planted dead center and making him appear even more regal and sophisticated as he scans the block for me. I had told him I would be getting ready at The Royale, and he expects me to be on foot for the short walk.

His eyes sweep out to the limo, then back down the block before returning to the limo as the door opens and I alight. His eyes flare with surprise, then he's moving toward me, the cane tapping on the sidewalk. It's an incredibly warm June evening, yet he looks dashingly cool and collected.

"Elena," he says in greeting as he offers me his arm. "That dress is stunning."

I flush with pleasure from the compliment. "It's Jorie's," I admit. "I can't afford the type of attire needed to attend these things. Luckily, we're the same size."

"Somehow, I don't think it would look as good on her," he says, paying me another gentlemanly compliment.

Again, it feels nice to have his acknowledgment. Still, I'd much rather have his grunts and groans, which speak more than his words. I fear I might have misplaced my priorities, but it's the truth.

Benjamin leads me into the casino, and we head toward the bank of elevators that will lead up to the event ballroom.

"So what is this event?" I ask.

"It's a fundraiser for the children's hospital," he replies.

"Do you come to a lot of these?"

We reach the elevators and he stabs at the button with his finger. "Not lately. Don't seem to have the patience for them anymore."

"So why are you attending this one?"

He grimaces. "Let's just say I owe a favor to my partner. And thank you for being my date."

I give him a wink and a lopsided smile. "Let's be honest... it was the prospect of going to The Wicked Horse with you afterward that made me agree."

His eyes round in surprise, his lips curving upward. "Really?"

"Really," I say with a firm nod of my head. "Why does that surprise you?"

He shrugs just as the elevator doors open. He ushers me in, and we move to the back as a handful of other people enter. He sidles in closer as the doors close and we start to ascend.

Leaning down, Benjamin murmurs, "Most single women just aren't into sex like that."

There's truth in his words. Most of the women at The Wicked Horse are in committed relationships. There is a lot of swinging that goes on with their partners. I have seen very few single women go there just for sex. On top of that, it's sad to say very few women can afford the fee.

I tilt my head up. He leans a little bit closer to me so I can whisper, "Let's just say I have found being involved in a committed relationship to be... un-empowering."

We reach our floor, and the elevator doors open. Benjamin moves me through the crowd, and we exit. I put my arm through his, and we head down the hallway to the ballroom where we can see people mingling.

"And yet," he says as we stroll along. "You give up all control to me. That doesn't seem empowering."

My laugh is husky, delighted. "On the contrary, giving up control is the height of empowerment for me. Knowing I've got the courage to do that, I mean."

Benjamin halts, and so do I. He turns, eyes quizzical. "You continually surprise me."

"Is that a good thing?" I ask.

He inclines his head. "It's an incredibly good thing. It's what I need."

Benjamin takes my hand in his, and we head into the ballroom. The soft strains of a waltz hit my ears and the smells of delicious food assault my nose, making my belly rumble. Benjamin nods toward a group of people and says, "Come on. I see Dr. Metzer there. He's the one putting on this gala. I need to say hello."

"Sounds good to me."

We maneuver our way over to the group. The surprised expressions on people's faces when they see Benjamin proves him showing up is unexpected. I guess it truly is unusual for him to attend these types of events.

I'm introduced to a portly older man—Dr. Metzer—who gives me a polite nod. Benjamin next introduces me to a very handsome man and his wife, Brandon and

Colleen Aimes.

"Brandon is my medical partner," Benjamin explains as we shake hands.

Brandon and Colleen look stunned to see me, and I wonder why. Does Benjamin not date at all? Is he gay? What if he has a wife... and I'm just a side piece he's brazenly parading around?

Those questions are all answered when Colleen seems to come to her senses and gushes, "It is so nice to meet you, Elena. It's nice to see Benjamin getting out for a change."

That puts me at ease, and I'm thankful it seems like I'll have someone else to talk to tonight.

"So, Elena," Brandon says. "What do you do?"

"I'm a hair stylist," I say, expecting a little bit of disdain over my lower-class status.

Instead, Colleen pipes up, "Here in Vegas? Because I'm looking for a change."

She pats her perfectly styled bob, tilting her head expectantly.

"In Henderson," I reply. "I actually own my own place there, but if you don't mind making the drive, I'd love to work with you."

"I can totally come to you," she chirps with excitement. "So how did you and Benjamin meet?"

I wasn't expecting this question. In hindsight, it was stupid not to expect it. I freeze, shooting a questioning look at Benjamin, who just stares back impassively, willing to accept whatever answer I give.

"An online dating service," I say as I turn back to Colleen.

She nods exuberantly. "That's all the rage these days, right? Swipe right. Or is it left? Regardless, I'm just thrilled Benjamin's out and about tonight. Oh, we should go get a table so we can sit together for when the auction starts."

"Why don't you grab us some seats?" Benjamin suggests to Colleen as he takes my elbow, making his intent to lead me away clear. "We're going to peruse the art pieces up for auction and grab a drink. Want anything?"

"We're good," Brandon says.

Benjamin takes it as an exit cue to lead me away. "Sorry about that," he murmurs as we meander through the crowd. "Didn't think to come up with a story about how we'd met."

"Well, what I said was sort of true."

He stops, turning to face me with a serious expression. "Look... I had thought I'd get you a room here tonight, so you don't have to drive all the way back to Henderson."

I look up at him, startled, the change of subject unexpected. "That's sweet, but unnecessary. I can stay at Jorie and Walsh's."

Benjamin looks slightly abashed as he reaches into his pocket and pulls out a key card. "Well, I sort of already got the room."

"Oh," I say, flushing deeply at the realization there is a room and a bed within close proximity to us. "What about The Wicked Horse?"

"I thought perhaps we'd just stay here. For convenience."

While The Wicked Horse provides all kinds of temptation and takes debauchery to the next level, the thought of perhaps spending an entire night with Benjamin is intriguing.

"Are you thinking what I'm thinking?" I ask.

His eyes flash. "What exactly are you thinking?"

"We go to the room right now. Unless, of course, you'd rather stay here and socialize."

Benjamin's lips curve in a sexy grin full of promise. "Let's go."

For someone who uses a cane to walk, Benjamin moves with surprising grace and efficiency as he leads me from the ballroom. A few people nod in greeting as he passes by, but he's moving with such purpose there's no doubt he doesn't intend to stop and engage.

I let him lead all the way to the seventeenth floor.

CHAPTER 9

Benjamin

I KNEW I'D hate coming here tonight, but I had to do it for Brandon. I hate the pitying looks I get from half and the glares of reproach I get from the others who think I've been too much of a dick the last year.

It used to be only pitying looks after the accident, but I wiped a lot of that away with my actions. I won't apologize, though. A single car crash with a drunk driver killed my wife and daughter. I'm beyond caring about apology.

I spent over a month in the hospital with a crush injury to my left leg, a collapsed lung, a ruptured spleen, and a hairline fracture to my left wrist. Another two weeks in a rehab facility for my leg. And yet another two weeks of outpatient therapy before I could return to work.

Miraculously, the fracture to my left wrist was clean and easily healed. I came out of the accident with my brain unscrambled and my hands still able to perform complex microsurgery. I should have been grateful for that, but I wasn't.

I was pissed at the world. At the drunk who ruined my life, at God for letting it happen, and at my friends and family who still had the gall to make me care about them, thus putting me at risk for bigger pain.

And venturing into this place tonight—with a beautiful woman on my arm and money to burn on a charity auction—trying to pretend like my life is normal and these things should bring me joy... well, it's all bullshit. It's not me anymore.

It's not like Elena was going to mind the hasty escape I just pulled. She'd told me she was all about the sex anyway. It's not like she wanted to hang out with me, Brandon, and Colleen, making cute small talk and nibbling on overpriced hors d'oeuvres.

Yeah... made sense to leave, and even better planning I'd thought to get a room for Elena. It truly was so she didn't have to make the drive back to Henderson tonight, but it will come in super handy right now.

Because the one thing I have just realized with utter clarity is Elena provides me an escape from the pain of my regular life. That was never more evident than just a few moments ago when I got annoyed by Metzer's smug smile and Colleen's hopeless romanticism I will find love again, and all I wanted to do was pull Elena out of there and lose myself in her. Probably would have fucked her right there in the elevator had we been alone.

As it is, the hallway leading us to our room isn't so short I can't enjoy the bit of anticipation. I hold onto her hand tightly, lest she think to bolt for some reason, and punch my cane down deeper into the plush carpeting with every step I take.

When I reach our room, I can't contain my need any longer. Whirling her around, I push her back into the door. Rather than open it, I press into her and slam my mouth onto hers.

Elena gasps, and I pull back briefly. Her eyes are wide with surprise, but there's also something deep within those chocolate depths that speaks to me.

Absolute fucking delight in my assault just now.

I groan, palming her face, and kiss her again. Elena's hands grip into the lapels of my tux, and she holds me tight. Her mouth is so fucking soft, lips full, and her tongue demanding.

Without thought, I put my hand on the neckline of her dress and pull it down on one side, exposing a plump breast with an eager nipple. I lift her tit, pushing it up as my head dips.

Elena's head falls back, knocking against the door as I pull her sweet nipple into my mouth to torture. Her hips rock into mine and her fingers dive into my hair, holding me tight.

She shifts, her hands tightening on my head. "Benjamin."

I ignore her.

"Someone's coming," she whispers. I ignore that, too. Don't fucking care.

Elena grips onto my hair, and she gives it a hard jerk to get my attention. When I lift my head, she's grinning with a slight tone of censure. She gestures, and I follow her gaze as she nods to the hall. An older couple, probably in their sixties, are walking our way, their own eyes pinned to the carpet. It's clear they got an eyeful already.

I'm not ashamed in the slightest, and I doubt Elena is either. We've both fucked in front of other people at The Wicked Horse, and exhibitionism is part of what gets us off. But I also don't want to get thrown out of this hotel.

Not bothering to fix her dress, I pull the card out of my pocket and punch it into the slot. When the lock releases, I'm pushing the door open and Elena through it. When I give one last glance to the older couple, I see the woman still has her gaze averted but the older man gives me a sly grin.

I slam the door in their faces.

Taking Elena by the arm, I escort her into the room. She gasps when I whirl her around a little roughly, my need for her all too apparent. Her eyes spark with lust and willingness.

Fuck, that's exactly what I need right now.

After I drop my cane on the bed, I move my hand to the back of her neck. I pull her to me for another rough kiss, then my fingers glide to her shoulder.

Putting the slightest pressure on her, I say, "Get on your knees."

Christ, my heart almost slams out of my chest when she smiles in a way that says, "It would be my pleasure."

Before her knees hit the ground, I'm working at my fly. My cock is already hard and needy. I have to push my pants to my hips to free it, and my gaze moves past its thickness to Elena's face just beyond as she stares up with patience from her kneeling position.

I stroke myself once, then rub the head of my cock over her lower lip. Her mouth parts, and her tongue comes out to touch me softly. It almost makes my legs buckle, having nothing to do with the weakness in my left leg. That's all her power and the way she wields it right now.

Elena's hands come up. One goes to my ass, then the other bats my hand away so she can take my length in her grip. She fists me tight, opening her mouth to receive me.

Fucking heat, wetness... so goddamn tight when she sucks me in. My jaw locks tight as my eyes close to savor the feeling for just a moment.

Only a moment.

I need to watch this.

I open my eyes, dipping my head to look down at her angelic face as I slide in and out of her mouth. Her cheeks hollow and her tongue flattens hard on the underside as she jacks me at the base with her hand while she sucks.

Fuck, she's a pro at this. It's something April never enjoyed doing—

I snap my eyes closed again, offering up a quick apology I'd even think of April right now. When I'm with another woman. That I'd dare to compare them.

My stomach turns, and I involuntarily try to pull away.

Elena doesn't let me, though. Her hand grips my base harder as she sucks me in deeper, giving a tiny growl of defiance I'd try to take this away from her.

"Fuck," I mutter, torn between the exquisite pleasure she's giving me and the notion I don't deserve this. This shouldn't be part of my life. I don't deserve to have anything that makes me feel this good.

Elena shifts, raising just a bit on her knees, and I let out a bark of surprise when she takes my cock in so deeply I'm pretty sure the narrow confines gripping me is her throat. I'm in so fucking deep her nose presses into my groin. She swallows, the muscles rippling across the head of my dick, and my balls start to ache with need.

She pulls back, a slow withdrawal of my cock coming out of her mouth, and I'm entranced again as I watch. Her hands move to my hips, glide around to my ass, then she presses her fingers to my muscles.

I'm unsuspecting when she pulls me hard against her, her mouth and throat opening for me as I disappear all the fucking way in again.

I go dizzy with how good it feels, and it will only take a few more pumps before I come. I could get on board with that.

Her fingers flex, digging into my muscles before sliding into the material of my boxers. She pushes downward, making room and freeing me. My cock comes out of her mouth, then she's nuzzling my balls with her lips.

Christ.

She licks them, pulls them into her mouth, and sucks gently and I'm having a crisis of faith in this moment. I'm not sure I've ever had a blow job this good.

She makes a deep sound of frustration, perhaps needing more. Her hands go back to tugging at my pants, then she's back on my dick. She grips my hips and, once again, she's using leverage to pull me into her throat. When she swallows, her muscles ripple around me.

Her hands move gently on my legs, sliding down, moving to the front and taking my clothing with her. She's expertly stripping me, and it's almost like a choreographed dance—she's that fucking good at it.

My heart stammers a moment when her fingertips encounter the top part of the scar on my thigh. She doesn't falter, only continues to explore my body at her leisure while she fucks me with her mouth.

I ignore her curious fingers running along the internal width of the scar. Ever so gently, she traces the bumps and ridges, but she never misses a beat while my cock moves in and out of her mouth, breaching her throat with every thrust.

And I am thrusting.

My hips are moving, and I can't help myself.

I cup her face, starting to pump into her. She stares with wide, trusting eyes while her fingers still move over my scar, then down the front of my thigh until she reaches the jagged point at the end just above my kneecap.

My breathing turns erratic as I concentrate not only on the feel of her, but also on the way in which she's letting me use her. Her mouth is an open vessel—her throat a private affair. And yet, she's granted me complete access.

Elena's hands slide to the back of my thighs. She shifts again, taking me in deeper.

"Going to come," I mutter, more to myself than for her benefit. I know without a doubt Elena would never want me to pull out.

As if to prove theory, she swallows me down deeper than before as she moans loudly. The vibrations skitter all over my cock, and it's my undoing.

My hands tighten on her face, my hips thrusting forward causing her to choke slightly, but then I hold perfectly still as I start to come into her throat. She swallows repetitively, drinking me down, and I swear I think I come a second time as another violent wave of pleasure hits me.

It seems to go on and on, my vision dimming a moment before turning brighter. The entire time, my eyes stay locked on Elena's, and she's staring with such intensity I swear a third shudder of ecstasy hits me.

"Fuck," I mutter, which seems to be about all the English language I can muster right now as I gently pull my hips back to withdraw from her mouth. Her hand comes up, delicately wipes at her lips and chin, and then she sits back on her haunches to smile in triumph.

She looks magnificent. Lips swollen and red, her breast still hanging out of her dress, and her eyes sparkling because that turned her on as much as it did me.

Quite sure it's not going to take much to coax another hard-on for me to fuck her.

Elena lifts a hand, reaches out, and touches a fingertip to my scar again. I freeze, not suspecting such a bold move now the haze of passion has dimmed a bit. Her eyes go there, and she once again traces the length of it as my pants are now pooled around my knees.

"What happened?" she asks as her gaze rises to meet mine.

"Car accident," I mutter, reaching down to pull my pants up.

"Don't," she murmurs, her hands moving to stop me. "You're beautiful, and I'd like to see more."

We engage in a staring contest, me gripping my

pants and her hands gently on mine.

"I mean," she continues in a cajoling tone. "You've seen me naked and well, I want to see you."

I swallow past the dryness in my throat, but no words come out. I have no idea what to say because what she's asking is very intimate.

It's not that I haven't shown my body at The Wicked Horse because I have. I've gotten naked in the middle of The Orgy Room, and I had a hedonistic fucking ball.

But those times before Elena, I didn't give a fuck what anyone thought of me. I didn't care if my scar turned them on or off, and I most certainly wasn't looking at their needs. Before Elena, it was all about just getting off.

It's different with her. I've found feeling in giving in to her. I was lost to the sensation the first time she came, and I realized it was a power that made me feel good.

She's aware of my indecision. I can see it on her face, along with a fortitude that scares me just a little.

With determination in her eyes, she pushes up from her kneeling position and steps into me. Her hand moves from mine, skims lightly upward along my thigh, and goes right back to my spent cock. It shouldn't have any life in it, but the minute her fingers close around it, it pulses from her touch.

Her head tips back, and she licks her lower lip. "Let's get naked, Benjamin, and explore each other's bodies. I promise you can do anything to mine you want."

My eyes flare, and she nods with a mischievous grin.

"Anything," she repeats. "It's yours."

Her fingers move to the buttons on my shirt, and she starts to undo them. The entire time, I don't take my eyes from hers. There's a strength in there I latch on to. For the moment, I'm going to give Elena exactly what she wants. I'll get naked with her, then I'll take what she's offering.

And it's been a long damn time since I've looked forward to something so much.

CHAPTER 10

Elena

MY PHONE ALARM goes off, and I shoot my hand out to turn it off quickly. I rub the sleep from my eyes, turning over in the bed to see if Benjamin is still there.

I half expected him to be gone but to my surprise, he's there. In the predawn gloom, I can just make out his naked form. He's sleeping on his back with one hand thrown carelessly above his head and the other resting on his ribs. He has one leg outstretched, the other bent, and he's breathing deeply.

His body is tremendously beautiful even with the grotesque scar on his left thigh.

He had said it was a car accident, and I hadn't asked for any details. It was clear to me that he was uncomfortable with it from the moment he tried to pull away from me to the way his eyes clouded over when I asked him what happened.

But we made it past that. I didn't care what caused it,

and it didn't change my attraction to him. What mattered was he gave me the same level of intimacy I'd given him. I wanted to see him naked, and he'd given it to me. Let me strip him down to nothing but his bare form. He was magnificent as he stood there for a few moments and let me run my hands all over him. It hadn't lasted long, though, because the more I touched him, the more excited he became. My clothes soon joined his on the floor, then he had me bent over one of the chairs as he fucked my brains out.

I stretch, raising my arms high above my head and lengthening my legs until my toes point. I feel quite luxurious despite how well used I am. Benjamin fucked me three times after that blow job. Three amazing, intense times where I let him use me however he wanted. I'm exhausted, yet exhilarated. Despite the lack of sleep, I feel damn good.

Something changed between Benjamin and me last night. Something seemed to break open within him after that blow job. Now, I know I've got some slick oral skills, but it was different with him. The things I did with my mouth were more intimate. Benjamin—being who he is—managed to push me past my own limits. Never have I held a man deeper within me, yet I feel like I could have taken him even farther. There is just no reasoning for it.

After that… after we got naked… we were both insatiable. Couldn't get enough of each other. We would fuck, doze off, wake up, then touch, kiss, and fuck again. It almost seems like a dream to be honest.

And despite the soreness between my legs, the lack of sleep, and the long workday I have ahead of me... I want him again.

Right now.

I scoot a little closer, gently resting my palm on his chest, which is moving with his deep breaths. Never have I connected sexually with a person like this. Even with all the kinky stuff I've done and the limits I push myself past, I've never felt so in tune with another human being.

I rub my thumb over his breastbone. It's like every touch is exactly where it's supposed to be, and he gives me exactly what I need when I need it. Even the pain he sometimes inflicts speaks to a need I didn't know existed within me.

I let my hand trail down his chest and onto his stomach. He clearly works out. I can see it in the lines of his form and lean muscles of his body. I'd noticed a small scar over his ribs last night, and I wonder if he got it in the same automobile accident.

The scarring on his leg is bad. I can't imagine how painful an injury like that must have been. He'd lost muscle and skin, and it wasn't easy to look at. But I had.

Every chance I could.

And I kept touching it so he could see it is a part of him I accept. That I'm attracted to. That deserves my attention.

I skim my hand down his stomach to the line of hair that leads to his soft cock, which is impressive in its length and girth while at rest. When it's hard, it's incredibly beautiful. Long and thick with a strong vein that runs on the underside. It stretches me, but it's also a perfect fit.

I have some time before I must leave. My first hair appointment isn't until ten AM. And as I said... I want Benjamin again.

Taking him into my hand, I start a light, sensual stroke. Within moments, his flesh responds. Slowly, it thickens and grows longer. I move over closer, go up on an elbow, and run my tongue down the length of it.

Benjamin shifts, and a low growl bubbles in his chest. I take him into my mouth, giving a gentle laving of my tongue around the head of his cock.

"What are you doing?" Benjamin asks gruffly, his voice heavy with sleep and growing lust.

I turn to look at him. "I'm doing you."

Benjamin lifts his head from the pillow. He chuckles... an oddly beautiful sound to come from such a quiet, serious man.

He doesn't say anything, but then again, he doesn't need to. His hand skims up the back of my thigh, over my ass, and then his fingers press into me from behind.

Oh, wow. That feels damn good. I'm instantly wet from his touch. Even though I'm a little sore, the pleasure far outweighs it.

Benjamin is fully hard within my hand, and I give a few firm strokes. Each time Benjamin takes me, he's always the one in control. I've not had any power. Not even that blow job because when push comes to shove, the way we ended that encounter was him full-on fucking my face as I just hung on for the ride.

That's okay. It's what I want.

But with this sexy man only half awake and on his back, I can't resist the opportunity to take what I want.

I surge up from the mattress, flip my leg over his lap, and straddle his erection. Planting one hand down into the mattress, I take him in my other and maneuver the head of him to my entrance. I bring my gaze up so I can look at Benjamin. He's staring at me with burning eyes. His hands move to my hips, and he hisses through his teeth as I lower onto his shaft.

So much beauty in the way I ride him. His face morphs, gentles, and then he lays his head on the pillow with his eyes closed. His hands hold tight to my hips, but he lets me set the pace. I work myself up and down, paying attention to every nuance flickering over his expression.

Benjamin drops a single hand, then presses his thumb against my clit. Pleasure shoots through me from the added sensation. Overstuffed with his beautiful cock and the pad of his thumb on my clit, I can't hold off the inevitable rush of pleasure I seek. I start bouncing hard, not able to contain the little mewling sounds coming out of me. Benjamin grunts and groans from the strain of pulling back his own orgasm. He bites straight teeth down into his lower lip, and his face looks gorgeously pained with the need to seek release.

I slam myself onto his cock, and with just a little bit of a harder push on to my clit with his thumb, I'm sent over the edge and screaming out my release. It triggers Benjamin's, and he grips me tight to hold me down while his hips surge upward in an explosive orgasm.

I collapse onto his chest, trying to catch my breath. Even though I can still feel the ripples of pleasure coursing through me, I already want him again.

That makes him dangerous to me. Like an addictive drug.

And yet, I'm not afraid.

Benjamin's fingers skim my forehead, moving hair out of my face. I crane my neck to look up at him, and he lifts his head from the pillow so our eyes can meet.

"Stay with me," he says softly.

"Stay with you?"

"All day. All night. Right here in this room. We'll fuck like animals, order room service, and then fuck some more."

Groaning, I let my head drop onto his chest. I wrap my arms tightly to his side, and it's not lost on me that he does not return the embrace. I take this only to mean Benjamin might not be much of a cuddler, but it isn't important to me. This is about sex and nothing else.

I lift my head, regret filling me. "I wish I could. But I have a full day of hair appointments."

He gives me a disappointed smile, but he nods in understanding. "Of course."

My return smile is lopsided. "If it helps… I would rather be here with you."

One corner of his mouth tips up. "It helps. Are you up for The Wicked Horse tonight?"

Now that has my attention. It would be a fantastic way to end the evening. "What did you have in mind?"

Giving me an evil smile, he shakes his head. "You'll find out when I want you to find out."

Damn, that is sexy. And now I really want him again.

But sadly, I have to get out of here. Long drive back to Henderson to shower, have breakfast, and then work. With a sigh, I press my lips to the base of Benjamin's neck, then pull off him before I can be tempted to start something else again.

CHAPTER 11

Benjamin

I T'S THURSDAY NIGHT. After four nights of consecutive trysts at The Wicked Horse, Elena is canceling this evening.

We've been together at the club every night since we stayed together at the hotel. It was a step I didn't ever envision taking with a woman. Sleeping all night together in the same bed is incredibly personal and intimate, and I probably would have thought twice about it that night except sleeping wasn't really on our minds. We kept fucking over and over again, not able to satiate ourselves.

It's hard on Elena to make it to The Wicked Horse every night. She has over a thirty-minute drive each way, plus she works eight-to-ten-hour days.

It's why I hadn't begrudged the text message she had sent me while I was meeting with a patient a little bit ago. We both decided to do away with the fantasy app for our communications. Sending text messages was just easier.

Admittedly, I was a little hesitant when she asked for my phone number so we could switch to text. I was fearful she might want to call me all the time, or she might read something into the fact we've exchanged phone numbers. But that didn't happen. The only thing she has done consistently since we exchanged our numbers is communicate with me about arranging meetings.

Exchanging numbers was not the only thing that changed. In the last four nights where we've met up at The Wicked Horse, we've started out in the Social Room to have a few drinks. It's not like we need them to unwind and relax. But that first night we met there after the hotel, I had a craving for a good scotch. I'd suggested a drink, and one led into two.

It was easygoing. Elena kept me entertained with stories about her clients—never divulging their names— as well as her family. She's the youngest of six and comes from a boisterous, obnoxiously close-knit unit. One night, as she sipped at a glass of wine, she warned me that her mother is Latina and her father was a combination of Greek and Dutch, and it made for weird emotions sometimes. She said she could go from weepy to pissed off in a nanosecond.

"It's a good thing we really click," she'd added. "I don't think you have to worry about pissing me off."

And she is correct.

We really do click. That's been apparent in the fact we continue to meet up for drinks each evening before we move deeper into the club to take our pleasure. The conversation has been easy and enjoyable.

I haven't had easy conversation in months and months. Not since before the accident. Why it's happening with this woman is beyond me. There is no doubt Elena and I share an incredibly special sexual connection. She has turned out to be the perfect woman for me in that respect. But the fact we can carry on conversation without making me feel trapped or guilty for doing so must say something.

I'm just not sure what—or if I want to give any credence that the phenomenon is because of her.

But tonight, she's begged off because she's exhausted. I don't question this in the slightest. She even admitted to me it was the drive that was weighing down on her tonight as she almost fell asleep on the road home last night. In her text, she said, *I just need to catch up on my sleep tonight. I'll be good to go tomorrow.*

I'm finished with my patients for the day. I have notes to dictate, and I need to review my records in the Harlan case since my ethics hearing is next week.

What I should do is text Elena to let her know it is all right and I'm eager to see her tomorrow night.

It is completely disconcerting to me that I instead pull up her number and initiate a phone call.

Elena answers on the second ring. "Well, this is a

surprise."

Yes, indeed. It is.

"I just wanted to let you know I totally understand why you're canceling tonight. I hope you're able to catch up on your sleep, so we can hook up tomorrow."

She gives a sigh of relief that comes through loud and clear over the line. "Thanks for understanding."

"I mean," I drawl in a teasing tone. "It's not like I arranged for two other guys to be with us tonight at The Wicked Horse. Three guys, and one of you. That could have been explosive."

Elena is silent for a moment before she asks in an inquisitive tone, "Did you really?"

"No," I drawl, then hesitantly ask, "But do you want me to?"

She and I have never once discussed exploring our sexual fantasies with another person. It happens all the time in the club. Hell, I've partaken in group sex there before. If I were a betting man, I would say Elena has before too.

"Actually," she rushes to say. "No. It's not really of interest to me."

The amount of relief that floods through me makes it clear why I never brought this up before. Because, apparently, there is no way in fucking hell I'm ever going to share her. It goes against everything in my nature to let another man touch her.

"You could come here... to my place?" she suggests.

"Your place?"

"Yeah… I mean, I don't have sex machines for us to play with, but I've got stuff. And I think we've proven we do vanilla just fine."

Now the long pause comes on my end. She has caught me completely off guard. I actually have to think a moment.

I would never invite her to my place because it's full of ghosts and weakness. But her place is a different matter, I suppose. It's no different than when we stayed together at the hotel, right? Even though our original arrangement was to meet at The Wicked Horse, it doesn't mean we are in any type of committed relationship if we go outside the club. So far, we've managed to keep a healthy distance from each other in all aspects of our lives except for the evenings.

"It's no big deal if you don't want to," she rushes to assure me, filling the void of silence. "Just a suggestion."

"No," I quickly say. "It's not I don't want to. I was just thinking about my schedule tomorrow. My first surgery is at seven AM."

She sounds disappointed when she says, "Oh, that's way too early. And I'd totally keep you up way too late if you came here."

"What if we just make it a very early night?" I suggest. "I can leave in about half an hour to come straight to your place. But I'm not staying all night. I can't trust you to let me sleep."

Elena laughs in delight. I love the deep, husky tones of it. More than anything, I love I made that sound come out of her.

"Okay," she says while still chuckling. "You can come here. And we will make it an incredibly early night. I'll kick you out of my bed as soon as we're done fucking."

"Can I pick up some food on the way?" I ask.

"Strawberries, chocolate, and whip cream. Two cans."

"On it," I say.

◆

"THAT WAS INTENSE," Elena drawls before rolling away from me to grab a strawberry out of the bowl on her bedside table. She takes a bite, then reaches out to plop the other half in my mouth.

We're both laying naked on her bed, having just recently reacquired rational thought and normal breathing after the amazing fuck we just had.

And she's correct… That was intense.

When she had led me back to her bedroom a bit ago, she had had a variety of toys laid out for my perusal. I'd grabbed a bottle of lube and one of her larger butt plugs. Her eyes got wide with awe and excitement.

I took my time getting her ass ready for it. Once I had that monster inserted firmly within, I fucked her slowly from behind, knowing every thrust put pressure on the plug. I lost track of how many times she came.

"You're very skillful with your fingers," she says as she rolls to her side to face me, plopping her head into her hand.

I laugh. "It's why I am a good brain surgeon, I guess."

"What type of surgery do you have tomorrow?"

"A craniotomy to resection out a suspected glioblastoma," I say grimly.

"That sounds serious," she replies softly.

I turn on my side to face her. "It is. The most aggressive form of brain cancer."

Her expression saddens.

"I don't understand stuff like that. So senseless, you know? I often question why God does that to people, but I know His plan is greater than anything I can hope to understand."

Yeah, I know all about senseless things, too. I don't respond to the God comment because he ceased to exist to me a long ago. Truthfully, I believe it's bullshit when people think God has a greater plan because there can never be anything good about taking the lives of innocents.

Elena leans over and presses a kiss to my shoulder, which I think is incredibly sweet. But then, she starts pushing me away with both hands, trying to force me across the mattress.

"Okay, get out of my bed. You gave me good orgasms, got a great one yourself from what I could tell, had ass play, which I don't just grant to anyone, and you have an early morning surgery tomorrow. So go... get out of here."

While I wasn't ready to leave yet, she's right. If I don't go now, I'll stay all night. We'll talk for a little bit more, then we'll fuck again. Probably doze off. Wake up. Fuck again.

If I don't go now, it's not going to happen.

I roll off the bed, chuckling, then make to grab my clothes from the floor. Kicking an empty can of whipped cream out of the way, I look back over my shoulder. She's laying there so unabashedly perfect, sexy, and fresh looking. Her smile is sweet even though she's a hellion in the bed.

I don't want to leave. I want to crawl back in bed, eat strawberries, and talk.

Fuck all night.

But I make myself go.

Because the fact I don't want to leave spells all kinds of trouble for me.

CHAPTER 12

Elena

"OKAY... I HAVE something to tell you."

"What?" Jorie demands.

"I met someone, and I want to get your advice on it, but I want to hear all about your doctor's appointment first."

Jorie rolls her eyes. "No. Tell me your thing first."

I shake my head adamantly. "No, it's not important. I only mentioned it to start off this lunch so I don't chicken out later and decide not to tell you. So I'm outing myself, which will ensure you hold my feet to the fire later."

Jorie just smirks. "You are so weird."

Grinning, I nod enthusiastically. "Right? But it works for us."

Her resounding laugh is from the belly. "Totally."

The waiter arrives, then sets down two glasses of ice water along with two paper-wrapped straws. We're regulars here at this establishment, so he knows we'll be ready to order. I always get the chicken salad, and Jorie fluctuates between a ham and cheese panini or a Cobb salad.

She surprises me and the waiter when she says, "I'll take the cheeseburger loaded, with extra fries on the side."

When our server is out of sight, I lean across the table and whisper, "You know you can't use your pregnancy to eat whatever you want, right?"

I get an exaggerated eye roll. "Yes, I know that, Mother. But I was a little too nauseated this morning to eat, and I'm starving now."

"Morning sickness?" I ask with concern.

She shrugs. "Who knows? Just because it's called morning sickness doesn't mean it necessarily happens in the morning. But it can start occurring at around six weeks, which is exactly where I am, so I'm assuming that's what it was. Which sucks. You know I'm such a sissy when I'm nauseated."

"Poor baby," I sympathize in a cooing voice. "Any other symptoms?"

Jorie being pregnant is fascinating since I've never had another friend go through this. Growing up and coming from a big family, I had always thought I would have a big family myself. Three, four, maybe five children. But since I've soured so much on what it takes to maintain a relationship, which isn't necessary but can be important in having children, that dream has sort of waned.

"My boobs are a little sore," Jorie says as she swirls her straw around in her ice water. "Have to keep reminding Walsh to be gentle with them."

"Just smack him hard on the head. After a few times, he'll remember."

We share a laugh, then Jorie proceeds to fill me in on everything she learned at her doctor's appointment earlier in the week. I'm fascinated when she explains her baby is the size of a pea, but at the end of the trimester, will be as big as a peach. The visual is helpful.

"So have you discussed names for the baby?" I ask.

I've got my own personal thoughts on it, but I expect they don't want to hear they should name their child, whether it be a girl or boy, after its godmother Elena.

"We've been discussing names since I threw away my birth control pills in Paris," Jorie says with a grin. "We both agree on the boy's name. Josiah Aaron."

My eyebrows slip upward. "It's kind of biblical."

"Weird, right? But we just started tossing names out of the blue. Weirdly, it sounded right to us both."

I shrug. "Whatever floats your boat. Although I think you should give careful consideration to Elena."

"For a boy's name?" Jorie asks with one raised eyebrow.

I don't answer her question, but rather blow her skepticism off with a wave of my hand.

"What about for a girl?" I stare pointedly, almost

daring her to throw out the name Elena.

She knows that's what I want, and she pointedly ignores me. "Walsh wants to name her Daenerys."

I blink at Jory. Blink again. A few more times.

She just stares back.

"Wait... from *Game of Thrones*?" I ask incredulously.

Jorie grimaces in pain. "Yup."

My chin pulls inward, and I shake my head. "I hope you nixed that."

She snickers loudly, then leans across the table toward me. "He thinks it will be cute. We can call her Dany. He wants her crib to look like a dragon."

"Your husband is twisted," I drawl in disbelief. "What do you want if it's a girl?"

Now is the time for her to seal our bond as best friends.

"Arya."

I frown. Not Elena? Not even something reasonable.

"From *Game of Thrones* again?" I ask.

"Yup."

"You are both entirely too weird for me."

Jorie snickers and I laugh, having had our fun. I truly don't care what she names the baby as long as he or she is happy and healthy.

After taking a sip of her water, Jorie gestures in a circular motion. "Okay, enough about baby names. Spill it on your stuff. What's going on?"

I poke my straw up and down in my water, watching

the ice cubes bob around. Where to begin? What to tell her without giving away too much?

"You're stalling," she presses.

I toss my straw down into the water, meeting her gaze. With a huff, I lean back in my chair and say, "Okay, fine… I'm sort of seeing someone."

As expected, this gets Jorie's attention. She shoots straight up in her chair, spine straight and eyes sparkling with interest. "Who?"

I give a wave of my hand. "No one you know."

That, at least, is the technical truth. She didn't know Benjamin when she saw him at her birthday party, and I doubt she knows him now.

"But that's not important," I continue before she can press me for details I don't want to give just yet, especially since he's a friend of Walsh's. "See here's the thing… well, he's sort of piqued my interest."

Jorie leans forward, resting her elbows on the table and putting her chin in the palm of one hand as she drawls dramatically. "Oh, do tell."

Her dreamy, hopeful expression has commenced.

"Well, he's the guy I hooked up with on the fantasy app at The Wicked Horse. Remember?"

She jerks in surprise. "Hot-wax guy?"

"Yeah, and well… we've been seeing each other pretty frequently since then. Mostly at the club, but he came out to my house last night."

This completely gets Jorie's attention because she

knows me well. Her eyebrows shoot straight up. "You let a man come to your house? The notorious 'I'm only in it for casual sex, and I'm a strong, independent woman who needs no one, hear me roar' person?"

Shaking my head, I try to explain. "It's not like that. He doesn't ask me for anything. He doesn't pull on me. In fact, I don't think he needs anything from me, including sex. I mean, he wants it... but I don't think he needs it. For some reason, that is so liberating."

The expression on Jorie's face transforms. It's like a light bulb went off within her. She's had an "aha" moment, which is why I decided to tell her a little bit about Benjamin. I knew she would eventually have some advice. "And that's why you like him. Because he's not showing any signs of codependency. He's a little aloof with you, right? Now you're even more intrigued by the man."

I nod, knowing she'd understand because she gets me. "But I keep waiting for the other shoe to drop. For his true colors to come out. Part of me wonders if he's pulling me in, making me drop my defenses, then, *boom*, before I even realize it, he'll be ensconced on my recliner, eating my food and telling me he lost his job but he'll find one soon."

Okay, I'm confident Benjamin would never do that. He's a neurosurgeon, for Pete's sake, but still... There are many ways to manipulate a woman other than just monetarily bilking them.

"So what's the problem?" Jorie asks, the confusion in her tone apparent. "I mean, you know the signs to look for. You know the losers. A lot of it usually has to do with socioeconomic background. The people who go to The Wicked Horse have money. I'm sure this guy you are seeing has money. You know he's not going to try to use you like that."

"I know," I admit. "But it's not always about money. It's about the draw on me and the pressure to be responsible for their happiness. With men, that's sometimes tied up in money and creature comforts. Other times, it extends to emotional manipulation. And yes, while I don't think this man needs me for that, it doesn't mean I won't be preyed upon."

Jorie leans forward with a serious expression. "You do realize not all men are like that, right? That there are some good men out there? Surely you can't be that jaded."

She makes a good point. With a sigh, I'm forced to admit it. "I do know that, Jorie. And I try not to be jaded. But it doesn't mean I'm not scared."

"Because you like this guy?"

"I'm not sure. I mean, on its face, all we really have is sex. Like great, phenomenal, mind-blowing, surreal sex. Which is all I ever thought I wanted, yet... I have to believe the reason it's so good is because there's an emotional connection. But how can that be? We don't do anything but have sex."

"But is that true? You just meet, have sex, and go on

your way?"

I give a half shrug. "I mean, it started out that way. Lately, though, we've been talking more. We even have drinks before we... um... you know, do our thing."

"Don't overthink it," she instructs. "Off the top of your head, what is it between you two that makes you think it's more than just sex?"

I wish I knew. When I replay our conversations, nothing seems apparent. But then something strikes me. It's not about words.

"I think it's the way he looks at me. Like I'm an angel or something. Like I make him reconsider what he thought he knew to be true."

Jorie reclines in her seat, crosses her arms over her chest, and nods. "There you go. Sometimes, it's not about what *is* said, but about what *isn't* said."

"I've never been *that* to anyone. Not truly, I mean."

"It sounds wonderful. Exciting. Thrilling."

"Scary," I add to her litany of positives.

"Maybe," she says with a smile. "But has that ever stopped you from doing anything before?"

"Not really."

"So ride it," she suggests emphatically, then her tone turns suggestive. "Ride him. See where it goes."

But I'll keep my expectations way down, I think.

Because, in my experience, even though Jorie got me to admit not all men are the same, I tend to attract a certain type. I'm not going to hold out hope that Benjamin will be different.

CHAPTER 13

Benjamin

THE DOCTOR'S LOUNGE at the hospital is no frills. There's a small kitchen in the form of a refrigerator, stove, a microwave, and a long counter with a sink. Upon the counter also rests a Keurig coffee maker. It's a place where the doctors can have some privacy while they eat a snack or a hasty meal, rather than using the hospital cafeteria. Because most of the doctors like to socialize, they'll often use the cafeteria, so this place tends to stay empty.

I'd sucked down two protein shakes I had brought with me this morning and I've got about another twenty minutes before my next surgery. I'm spending the better part of my time scrolling on my phone and thinking of Elena.

Last night at her house was fun, and that's not something I've had a lot of lately.

Let's face it… the sex was the best part. But there was actual joking and laughing while we played with strawberries and whipped cream. It was fun, jovial, low pressure, and sticky.

And I didn't want to leave, goddamn it. I wanted more time with her. I'm not sure if it was for the sex or the laughter or perhaps even both. But it took a lot of effort to walk out of her place.

The point is, I'm starting to feel again. While it's scary as fuck, I admit I like it.

Admit I've missed it.

Every moment I spend with Elena feels like I'm walking through a tunnel with her. There's a light at the end. Every time we fuck, laugh, kiss, stare at each other... the light gets brighter and brighter. The moments with her lead me closer to it.

After I had woken up this morning and gotten out of the shower, I checked my text and was pleasantly surprised to see one from her.

I feel so refreshed after a good night of sleep last night. I am so ready for you in the WH tonight.

There was no stopping the smile that came to my face. The joy that bubbled inside, knowing that in less than half a day, I would be in her presence again.

Can't wait, I typed back.

I went to set my phone down so I could get dressed, but she immediately responded. It didn't irritate me, nor did it feel like she was taking up my time. I snatched the phone back up, eager to see what she would say. *Thought maybe we could invite another woman or two to join us tonight.*

A jolt went through my body at what she was suggesting, but I had to take a moment to think about it. Let's face it... there's not a man I know who would turn his nose up at such an offer.

And yet, after a bit of thought, I texted back, *Not interested.*

Not even a little, I realize.

There have been a few occasions at The Wicked Horse where I've had two women at the same time. It was fun. I got my rocks off.

But I'm not interested now. I only want Elena. I don't know if it means forever because that would be a poor bet to make in my situation. But that's the way it is now.

She responded, *Good answer. See you tonight.*

Yes, she would. I'm thinking we are long overdue for a little bit of exhibitionism. While everything we've done lately at the club has been outside of the private rooms in The Apartments, I was thinking of a bigger display. Maybe one of the new sex machines Jerico put in at The Silo. Or maybe I'll get her off with my hand in the Social Room. Sex is not off-limits there, but it usually doesn't happen. It would guarantee many eyes would be on us. I can certainly say it appeals to my ego, having everyone watch and knowing Elena is mine... if only for a moment.

Two vaguely familiar doctors walk into the lounge.

Orthopedics, I think. A man and a woman who are chattering away.

Based on purely a glance, I can tell by the expressions on their faces that my reputation of being an asshole precedes me. They try to avoid eye contact, but not before I give them an engaging smile. They blink, jaws dropping slightly, before hastily turning away.

I snicker, getting a little bit of amusement over how discombobulating a smile can be.

The two doctors grab their food out of the refrigerator, then move clear across the room to sit away from me. The lounge is still small enough I can clearly hear them as they start talking.

I continue to scroll through my phone and eavesdrop, because I've got nothing better to do. I need to push my thoughts of Elena aside, otherwise I'll be walking through the hospital corridors with a hard-on.

The male doctor launches into a complaint I only half pay attention to. It has to do with his ex-wife.

Whatever.

"I had it all planned out," he tells the female doctor. "I was going to take him fishing. I requested this weekend off eons ago, and she agreed to it. And now she's saying I can't have him because it's not my normal weekend."

So much drama. Rolling my eyes, I turn over to the weather app to look at the forecast for the next few days. I was thinking about getting my boat out of storage to take it out on the lake. Maybe I'll even invite Elena.

"I'm so sorry," the female doctor says in commiseration. "Of all the weekends she would do this to you."

"Right?" the male doctor demands. "Father's Day should inherently go to me, don't you think?"

My entire body locks tight, and I look over at the doctors. Father's Day?

I didn't know that. Had no reason to. I don't pay attention to holidays these days. I only look at my surgical schedule, my patient schedule, and that's it.

Father's Day.

I'd only celebrated five with Cassidy. Last year, I'd still been immersed in closing myself off from the world, doing outpatient rehab, and working insane hours. I hadn't even known what had happened. Looking back, I'm quite sure most people made sure to stay clear of me, making sure not to mention it.

If these two fuckers hadn't walked in, I probably would have been oblivious about it this weekend, too.

I'm not prepared for the overwhelming sadness sweeping through me. I've managed to put Cassidy out of my mind for the most part, and I'm not quite prepared to handle the resurgence of her memory. The mere thought of what I will never have with her again is crushing. I had moved her and April into my "past life," where I keep them securely tucked away and treasure them from afar. I've had to accept I had five amazing years with Cassidy and nine with April, but that time is over now.

It's fucking over, and I'll never feel Cassidy put her hands on my face and whisper, "I love you, Daddy, to the moon and back," or have her crawl in bed with me and April on a Saturday morning to cuddle and watch cartoons, or ask me to fix her little scrapes with Band-Aids because I'm a doctor and Mommy isn't, and—

The pain hits me like a burning fire through every molecule of my body. Worse than I ever felt when my mom first told me April and Cassidy had died. At least back then, I was under the heavy influence of narcotic drugs to dull my physical pain. It had made it a little bit easier to cope with the devastating news.

But now, this pain is oppressive, and I feel like I'm drowning. It's even worse than how I felt when the judge convicted Pettigrew and sent him to prison for killing my family. He hadn't shown a shred of remorse. I'd wanted to kill him, but I couldn't. It had hurt so bad I'd never wanted to feel pain like that again.

But right now? Thinking about Father's Day, how I'm all alone, and how Cassidy is dead makes me feel like I might be dying right now. The pain is that devastating.

"Fuck," I mutter as I push up quickly from the table. The plastic chair I'd been sitting in flips backward. The other two doctors look concerned, but they don't say a word.

I stumble past the table, then out of the lounge. I don't even know where I'm going. Walking like a drunk, I careen off walls. Suddenly, I realize I left my cane back in the lounge.

Fuck it.

There's a men's bathroom up ahead. I push through the door, stumbling toward the sink. After I turn the cold water on, I throw handfuls of it into my face, realizing I'm gasping for breath.

Panicking.

I don't how to deal with this pain.

"Goddamn it," I roar as I stare at my reflection in the mirror. A crazy man glares back. "Get a fucking grip, Benjamin."

Squeezing my eyes shut, I take several deep breaths. I will myself to move past the panicky feeling of losing everything that is important in my life again.

Why is this happening? Why now?

I suck in another deep breath, holding it deep in my lungs until my eyes start to water from the effort, then I let it back out slowly. When I force myself to look at my reflection again, the answer is clear.

This is happening because of Elena. She had opened me up.

Made me reach for possibilities.

She'd burrowed her way into my life, and I'd thought she might be an angel sent to rescue me.

A mirthless laugh erupts from within me. I give myself a chastising head shake in the mirror.

"She's no angel," I tell myself. "Because there is no God."

CHAPTER 14

Elena

I CAN'T TELL if I'm worried about Benjamin or pissed at him. We were supposed to meet up at The Wicked Horse night before last, but he hadn't shown up.

Hadn't called.

Hadn't texted.

Of course I reached out to him. I felt like an idiot, waiting at the bar in The Social Room for him, fending off other men's advances while I sipped on a glass of wine. I texted him and when he hadn't responded, I'd called. I'd gotten his voice mail.

Benjamin is a punctual man, so when he'd been twenty minutes late with no word from him, I'd known he wasn't coming. I didn't even finish my wine—just threw a five-dollar tip on the bar top and left. It never occurred to me to stay and enjoy myself with someone else, because Benjamin and I had agreed to be exclusive. At that point, I was more worried than anything.

Of course I thought the worst. Car accident, mugging, or brain aneurysm. For all I knew, he could be dead somewhere and I wouldn't even know what happened. We weren't close enough I could just jump in my car and drive to his house to check on him. I had no clue where he lived.

So I went home, had another glass of wine, and went to bed. I'd slept horribly all night, tossing and turning as I wondered what happened to Benjamin.

My worry on Friday gave way to anger on Saturday. I had to work all day, and I stewed over how he could so rudely stand me up. Based on the nature of the things we'd done together, he at least owed me a simple, "It's been fun, Elena, but it's time to move on." Without those words, he'd left me in a state of worry. And it pissed me off even more. By Sunday morning, I was back to worrying. When I really thought about it, him just breaking it off made no sense. Sometimes, I'm not the best judge of character when it comes to men, but I hadn't imagined there was something deeper between us. It was something I have never felt with another man. Call it chemistry or primal attraction, but it was something so unique I can't just dismiss it.

I put on the finishing touches to my makeup—some pressed powder and lip gloss—and smooth my dress down. I'm practically on my way out the door to meet my parents for church, but I still have a few minutes I could spare.

Nabbing my phone, I call Jorie, because it's time to

employ my bestie for what she does best—giving solid advice.

"What's up?" she answers on the second ring. She and Walsh don't go to church, so I feel slightly guilty I might be messing with a lazy Sunday morning for them.

"I need your help," I say as I move through my house, turning off lights and the TV. "Well, Walsh's to be more accurate."

"Walsh's?" she asks in surprise.

Guilt flushes through me, and I know it's time to fess up. "You know the guy I've been seeing?"

"Hot-wax dude," she replies knowingly.

"Yeah, well... his name is Benjamin. You can call him that now instead of 'hot-wax dude'. But anyway, he's the one who was at your birthday party."

"I'm confused." And I knew this would take some explaining, but I try to let her work out as much as she can. "I thought you met him at The Wicked Horse."

"I did, but he was coincidentally at your party."

"And you didn't bother to tell me this why?" she demands hotly, although I know she's not angry. Just a little miffed I've withheld.

Sighing, I hold my phone between my shoulder and my ear so I can take stock of the contents of my purse to make sure I don't need anything else. "I'm sorry. I just sort of wanted to keep him to myself for a while. He's a little mysterious, intense, and, well, different from anyone I've ever known."

"You could have told me," she sniffs.

"I'm telling you now. I need your help because I'm worried. He sort of went off the grid. Stood me up Friday night, and I haven't heard from him since."

"And you've tried to call him?"

I roll my eyes, knowing she can't see it, so I make sure she hears it in my tone. "Of course I called him. A few times. Texted, too, but he hasn't responded. I was wondering if Walsh has any insight he can offer. I have no clue how close their friendship is, but I thought maybe fairly close since he was at your party. I'm operating in the dark here, and I just can't let it go."

"Elena," Jorie says softly, dropping her voice an octave. "Are you sure you haven't been dumped in a fantastically assholish manner?"

That's a legit concern. As my bestie, I'd expect her to consider these things and make sure I am, too. "Ordinarily, I'd say yes. But, in this instance, my gut is saying it's something else. I just need to know."

"Okay, then." Her tone is decisive, and she's fully in. "Let me go get him."

It's silent for a few moments. I use the time to grab my keys and head for the door.

I'm just locking it closed behind me when she comes back on. "I've got Walsh on speakerphone. I've filled him in a bit."

"So you're dating Benjamin Hewitt, huh?" Walsh says, and I don't like the tone of his voice. I thought he'd tease me first, but he sounds worried.

"I'm not sure dating is the word," I reply hesitantly. "It's sort of a Wicked Horse kind of thing, but there was a real connection there. I'm worried because he just sort of dropped off the face of the earth. I'm hoping you can give me some insight."

"You know about the accident, right?" Walsh asks.

My brow furrows at this odd question. "The one that injured his leg?"

"It was a bit more than that," he says in a sad voice, and my stomach clenches. "His wife and daughter were killed. He was seriously injured. Spent a really long time in the hospital."

"What?" I rasp, feeling incredibly dizzy by this revelation. I had no clue, and I feel like reality slapped me with a cold, wet washcloth or something.

"A drunk driver crossed the center line and hit their car head-on."

"He had a wife and daughter?" I murmur, voice barely audible.

"It fucked him up in the head. I mean, he's no longer the guy I used to know. Frankly, had I known you were seeing him, I would have discouraged it."

There's censure in his tone. I imagine he's giving Jorie the side-eye right now for keeping this secret, but he has no clue she didn't know. I'll fix that later.

Walsh isn't finished making his point. "He's not a nice guy, Elena. Can't say we were the best of friends before his accident, but we hung out. Golfed together a lot. Some poker nights. He came out of that accident completely changed. Closed himself off from everyone."

The information is overwhelming, but it doesn't discourage me. If anything, I feel more of a pressing need to make sure he's okay. "Do you know where he lives?"

His tone is apologetic. "I don't."

"It's okay," I reply glumly as I move to my car.

"What are you going to do?" Jorie asks, her question laced with equal amounts of curiosity and worry. She knows me well enough to know I'm not going to do nothing.

"Call him again after church," I reply on a sigh. "Probably head to The Wicked Horse tonight to see if he shows up."

"Just be careful," Walsh advises.

"Wait!" Jorie exclaims with mild panic. "Is this guy dangerous or something? If so, you cannot go to The Wicked Horse to see him. Stupid idea. You probably need to let this go."

I can hear Walsh chuckling, and I imagine his arm going around Jorie. "Ease up there, mama bear. I don't mean for Elena to be careful because Benjamin is dangerous or anything. I just mean he's got a lot of baggage. Does she really want to get caught up in all that?"

The answer is a resounding "no." I don't want to be caught up in that. It's the story of my life with men. I end up taking care of them, helping to figure out a way to battle their demons. I'm done being the fixer of broken men, and yet... I can't lie... I'm still pulled toward this man.

I wish I could put my finger on what this is. Why am I feeling such a strong pull to someone who just spells bad news all the way around?

The most I can do is try to reassure Jorie and Walsh. "I'll be careful, I promise. I just really want to make sure he's okay."

And once I discern whether he is, I'll need some validation I wasn't misreading the connection I thought we had. It's fine if he wants to call it quits because he's not emotionally ready, but I need to know I haven't been imagining things.

CHAPTER 15

Benjamin

I T'S FATHER'S DAY, and there's nowhere for me to hide.

I started the day off by taking my boat out to the lake. It was swarming with families—kids everywhere—and I realized it was a horrible mistake right away. I never even bothered to put my boat in the water.

After I left there, I decided to go hiking, figuring I might get lucky enough for a rattlesnake to bite me—maybe put me out of my misery. I'd never noticed it before, but hiking was apparently a fun and popular family event. Again, more reminders of what I no longer have, so I hadn't even bothered to get out of my car.

I'd driven off, then ended up at some strip club. So I sit here drinking as I watch the women dance. It does nothing to take my mind off my daughter. Copious amounts of alcohol, undulating tits, and shaking asses as far as the eye can see, and all I can think about is how terrified Cassidy must've been at the moment of impact.

She wasn't killed right away the way April mercifully was. Cassidy had suffered before she died. It's unbearable to think about, and I need something different to occupy my mind.

I'm stinking drunk when I leave, but all I've lost still swarms through my mind. Regardless, the one thing I will never, *ever* do is drink and drive, so I ditch my car at the strip club and take an Uber to The Wicked Horse.

I park my ass on a barstool in The Silo, which is usually where the kinkiest shit happens. No one here sparks a desire in me, though. Nothing I've seen has inspired me at all. Not even managed to get a tiny thump from my dick.

At least I'm not thinking about Cassidy… much. I suspect it's the combination of my inebriation, along with the wide array of sex acts going on all around me that is keeping my mind occupied.

A large hand comes down on my shoulder and I turn to see Jerico Jameson, the owner of The Wicked Horse, seating himself on a stool to my right. I lift my chin in acknowledgment before swiveling to hunch protectively over my drink, hoping my body language indicates I'm not in the mood to be social.

"If you're looking for Elena, she doesn't come in on Sundays. She spends it with her family," Jerico says in a matter-of-fact tone.

I tip my head his way again, slightly surprised he would bring her up.

"You seem to know an awful lot about your customers," I observe, noting my slurred speech since it gives away the extent of my inebriation. It's the first time I've spoken to anyone tonight other than to order a drink from the bartender.

Jerico shrugs. "Not all of them. But Elena's special."

There is no stopping the glare I shoot his way. His tone was way too intimate when he speaks her name, and I don't like it.

Jerico laughs, holding his hands up in mock surrender. "I only meant she's best friends with the wife of one of my former customers who still remains a good friend of mine."

"Walsh Brooks," I mutter in acknowledgment.

Jerico nods and motions to the bartender, holding up two fingers and then pointing at himself and then me. He turns my way. "You know him?"

"We used to golf together," I say curtly as I drain my drink in preparation for the one Jerico just ordered for me. "Anyway, I'm not here looking for Elena. It didn't work out between us."

Just uttering those words causes a wave of longing to hit me. I may have cut her out of my life, but it doesn't mean I don't still want her.

"That surprises me," Jerico murmurs. "You two were the talk of the club. Your chemistry was off the charts. I'd even observed you two together a few times. You had something special there."

His words hit me hard. I don't need him to tell me there was something special there. I fucking felt it.

I refuse to acknowledge it, though. "Not really. She was just a good fuck."

Pain pinches at the center of my chest—a sure sign of the guilt I feel for even saying that. She was so much more than a good fuck, which is exactly why I had to cut her loose. She was making me feel way too much, and I am just not ready for that.

The bartender brings our drinks. As I reach for mine, Jerico firmly states, "That's your last one of the evening. You know we have a two-drink maximum."

"Already drunk," I mutter, but then I raise my glass and offer, "Thanks, though."

"If you don't mind me saying so," Jerico starts as he leans an elbow on the bar, "you seem like a man who has a lot weighing on him."

I give him a sharp look, hating his perceptiveness, but I quickly look away again lest I acknowledge just how right he is.

He's not deterred. "Not trying to pry into your business. I'm just saying... I know the look of someone who comes in here to lose themselves in pussy or cock or whatever floats your boat. Yet, nothing is interesting you tonight. So why even bother?"

I look around The Silo. It's the usual kink. A threesome going in one room, a woman getting flogged in another. Two guys sixty-nining in yet another room.

My attention returns to Jerico, and I can't even be mad at his nosiness. On the contrary, the alcohol seems to have completely killed my desire for misery and privacy. "Today is Father's Day, and I'm trying to forget my five-year-old daughter is dead. I've tried several places to forget about her, and I figured somewhere like this was my best chance. It seems to be working."

Jerico's expression softens. "I'm deeply sorry, Benjamin. I didn't know."

I shrug. "Few do. It's not like I talk about it."

This morning, I had briefly wondered if I should visit Cassidy's grave. I had thought I should spend Father's Day with her, but I couldn't bring myself to do it. I didn't want to set precedence for this holiday. Who knows... maybe this will be my precedence? Losing myself in a sex club and alcohol to avoid the pain.

"Did it work?" Jerico takes a sip of his drink, his gaze heavy on me. "Does the stuff in here get your daughter off your mind?"

"A little bit," I admit. I pick up my drink, then take a healthy slug of the bourbon Jerico bought me. It doesn't even burn going down anymore.

"Is that why you started coming here? To shut yourself off from everything that happened?"

My laugh is mirthless and flat. "Actually, just the opposite. I've done such a good job refusing to think about them while shutting myself off from any reminders that I became numb to everything."

Jerico jerks in surprise. "Them?"

"My wife died, too. Drunk driver hit our car."

"Jesus Christ," Jerico mutters, then takes a large gulp of his own drink. I'm aware of how pathetic it sounds.

But the alcohol and Jerico's persistent questions have loosened my tongue. "I spent months burying them... the memory of them at least. It was too painful to even think about. But I got so good at it I wasn't feeling anything. I thought coming here would at least let me feel physical pleasure. At least that was something."

An expression takes over Jerico's face, like a lightbulb going off. "Then you met Elena Costieri, and it was all over. No more burying the pain."

I don't like the importance he is placing on Elena. It only adds to my guilt over what I did. I'm in denial when I say, "It wasn't like that at first."

"But it did turn into something," Jerico says sagely. His words ring with empathetic truth. I can't even be annoyed he's trying to play psychologist with me.

"She opened me up," I admit grudgingly. "She left me vulnerable."

Jerico nods, as if he's heard the sad tale before. But in truth, it's not that hard to connect the dots about my story. "Let me guess... Father's Day came along, Elena had opened you up, and the pain hit you extra hard?"

"You don't know the half of it," I mutter, swallowing down the rest of my drink and pushing the empty glass toward the edge of the bar. The bartender doesn't even spare me a glance; he knows I'm cut off. "I was sitting at the hospital on Thursday, and I just happened to overhear a conversation about Father's Day. I didn't even know it was coming up. I normally ignore that shit. And yeah... it dredges up all the stuff I had worked so hard to bury."

"And?" Jerico just stares.

"And what?"

"How does Elena play into all of this?" he asks simply.

I frown. "Well, it's her fault, isn't it? She's someone I can't stay closed off from. I should have known better than to ever get involved with someone like her. But that's done now."

"Just dumped her, huh?" The condemnation in Jerico's tone is clear, meaning he has some affection for her.

"Something like that," I mutter guiltily.

Jerico straightens, slaps a hand on the bar, and pins me with a hard look. "That was a dick move, Benjamin. I don't care what your emotional trauma was."

"Yeah, I know. But it's for the best. It was never going to go the distance anyway."

"Guess you'll never know," Jerico drawls, and there is something ominous about the way that sounds. As if my last little bit of hope has just slithered away. Even if I hadn't realized I'd had a kernel of hope left until that very moment.

"I guess not," I murmur pensively.

"Can I ask you a question?" Jerico inquires politely.

"Shoot," I reply slowly, my tongue so thick it's almost hard to get the word out.

"The pain you felt on Thursday... in the hospital when you overheard the conversation about Father's Day? I assume it hit you pretty hard to have just broken things off with Elena."

"It's the worst I've felt in a long time."

"Tell me honestly... do you feel that bad right this moment? I mean, despite the fact you're drunk as a skunk and alcohol is a downer, but comparing the pain... how does it feel?"

"It's not as intense," I admit. "I've had a few days to process. What's your point?"

Jerico leans into me, locking his eyes on mine. "My point is that between Thursday and now, you seem to be handling it. You're coping. Drinking, but coping. Grief is necessary, but the pain always gets better. You've made it through the worst, Benjamin. And that has nothing to do with you cutting Elena out of your life."

I just blink at him, trying to process what he's saying through my inebriation.

It's as if he can see I'm not following, so he simplifies it for my drunk, simpleton mind. "Don't let something good slip away just because there's risk."

I stare, knowing in a world of common sense and rational thinking that he's right. Any sane and sober person would think so.

Jerico doesn't expect an answer from me. He pats me on the shoulder, gives me a nod, and walks away.

I let my eyes drift over to the glassed-in room where the threesome is still fucking. I take in the beauty and sensuality of the act. Man on his back, woman riding him, and another man behind her plowing her ass.

Mercifully, I'm not thinking about Cassidy, April, or Elena anymore... and that's something at least.

CHAPTER 16

Elena

I REALLY DO have better things to do with myself on a Monday. The salon is closed, and it's usually my day to catch up on bookwork, inventory, and any personal errands. That I am instead at Benjamin's medical practice is most likely a total waste of my day.

I simply can't help it, though. I'm really concerned about him—also very pissed—but I'm more worried than anything. Now that I know about his horrible history... his wife and daughter dead... I can't help but be fretful for his welfare.

After talking to Walsh and Jorie, there was no stopping my need for more details. I had to Google the news story of Benjamin's accident. It seems as if they were driving one evening when a drunk driver who had two prior DWIs crossed the centerline and hit them head-on. His wife, April, had been killed upon impact. Their five-year-old daughter Cassidy had a major brain injury—the irony of which cannot be lost on anyone given what

Benjamin does for a living—and was taken off life support a mere twenty-four hours later.

The news articles did not give much detail about how serious Benjamin's injuries were, but I suspect it was much worse than what happened to his leg.

I don't know the exact why of it, but it's obvious the accident and their deaths have everything to do with why he cut me off without a word. And because I know deep down in my gut—really, my heart—that we had a solid connection, I just can't let this go. I must find out why he did this *when* he had, and I have to make sure he's going to be okay. In the brief time we've known each other, I have come to care about him. It doesn't matter that our relationship revolves only around sexual gratification, the level of intimacy we have shared and knowing what I now know about his history has unfortunately caused my heart to become involved.

There is no doubt what I'm doing would be considered stalkerish. I showed up at his place of work this morning, then walked confidently up to the reception desk. His offices are on the fourth floor of a large glass medical building right beside the hospital. The interior is posh with expensive furniture and high-end art. It's no secret neurosurgeons are at the top of the pay scale when it comes to the medical profession. And yet, nothing about the fact he is wealthy appeals to me.

Unfortunately for my quest, the receptionist shut me down cold.

"Yes, I would like to see Dr. Hewitt," I told her with confidence.

"Do you have an appointment?" she asked with a friendly smile.

I shook my head. "No. But I'm a friend of his."

The friendly smile slid off her face. There is no doubt their protocol required people to have an appointment to get precious minutes with the neurosurgeons here. "I'm sorry, but if you don't have an appointment, you cannot see him."

I'd expected as much. While she did promise to leave him a message, I seriously doubted it would make it into his hands. I also suspected he would ignore it, but it's important I catch him face to face to get a serious answer to my questions.

I didn't give up, though. I merely walked through the lobby and out the door, where I have been loitering in the hallway for going on almost two hours now. It is my hope I will catch Benjamin coming out on a break.

Leaning against the wall with one foot propped against it, I surf my phone and bide my time. Periodically, I push away from the wall and pace up and down the hallway. At one point, I risk a bathroom break, rushing back to my post so I don't miss Benjamin.

My phone dings, and I look down to see a text from Jorie. *What are you doing today?*

For a moment, I consider being evasive with her. But since she and Walsh are extremely concerned about me and my relationship with Benjamin, I opt for the full truth. *Stalking Benjamin at his office.*

She texts back an emoji with wide, disbelieving eyes.

I type back to explain further. *I just want to make sure he's okay since he's not returning my calls or texts.*

With Jorie, I know I can always count on her for the hard truth. For honest advice. She's the one to tell me when I'm being stupid or ridiculous. I sort of expect that from her, so I'm surprised when she merely replies, *Good luck. Call me after you talk to him.*

That makes me feel immensely better about my decision to come here. I have been second-guessing myself somewhat that maybe some people are just better off left alone. Unfortunately, I am a naturally empathetic person and my sleepless nights will continue until I can assure myself Benjamin will be okay.

"Elena?" It's a man's voice—clearly not Benjamin's—and I snap my head to the left to see his partner, Brandon Aimes, walking toward me. He's wearing a set of blue scrubs, carrying a few Manila medical files under his arm. I'm surprised he remembers my name. "What are you doing here?"

His tone is friendly enough, but his expression is wary. I wonder if Benjamin has said anything about standing me up last week.

Lifting my chin, I tell it straight. "Benjamin and I had a date on Friday, and he stood me up. He's not been returning my calls or texts, and I am very worried about him. I just want to make sure he's okay."

"He's actually not here," Brandon replies as he comes to a stop before me.

I cock an eyebrow. "The receptionist made it seem like he was. She asked me if I had an appointment."

"That's what they're trained to say. They're also trained to never divulge where the doctors are. She would've tried to get you in to see another one of our doctors."

I suppose that makes sense.

Brandon looks up and down the hall before turning back to me. He seems troubled about whether to say anything, but he eventually sighs and admits, "Look... he left work on Friday around lunchtime, skipping out on a surgery he had scheduled. I was able to cover it for him, but it was completely unlike him to do something like that. Today, he called out again, but he assured me he would be back tomorrow."

I don't know what to make of that. It hits me with a harsh clarity I simply don't know Benjamin well enough to know whether his behavior is unusual or worrisome.

"Well," I drawl hesitantly. "I really just wanted to make sure he was okay. Since you've heard from him, I guess I've been assured of that. Thanks."

I am feeling extremely dissatisfied with what I've learned, but I don't feel like I have any choice but to walk away. My goal was to make sure Benjamin was physically okay. Brandon has heard from him, and it appears Benjamin is. I give him a smile and pivot on my foot, heading toward the bank of elevators.

I don't make it three steps before he calls after me, "Elena… wait a minute."

I spin to face him.

"I'm not sure he's okay," Brandon admits, and I take a few steps toward him. "He's probably going to kill me for this, and I have no clue of knowing if you're legit or a crazy stalker woman, but I'll take my chances."

Brandon pulls a prescription pad out of his front pocket along with a pen. He's scribbles something down, tears it off, and hands it to me.

After I take it, I look down. Benjamin's address.

I blink in surprise, feeling immediate relief I can go see him.

"I am not a crazy stalker," I assure him. "I promise. I just… I think we had a connection and he got scared or something. I just need to make sure he's okay. See if there's anything there."

Brandon appraises me a moment before nodding. "I saw it."

"What's that?"

"The connection. Brief as it was, he let me see it the night he introduced you to us at the gala, I could tell there was something there. It made me happy."

I drop my gaze to the floor, and shuffle from foot to foot before looking back up to Benjamin's medical partner. "I just found out what happened. The accident.

And how his wife and daughter died. I didn't know it at the gala. Well... I can't help but think it has everything to do with why he stood me up on Friday. I just can't figure out why now."

"He's prickly about it," Brandon says neutrally.

"Prickly?"

Brandon gives a short chuckle. "Okay, he's an asshole actually. After the accident, he became a different man. He cut everyone out of his life who ever meant something to him. Me, his parents, his brother. He rarely talks to us. All he does is work and sleep. That's about all there is to his life. That's why I was glad to see him bring you to the gala. It gave me hope."

I'm shaken to the core by this information. It means Benjamin is pretty far gone from being a normal human being. It makes me doubt the connection I thought I felt. "We just fuck."

Brandon's face turns red at my coarse words, his eyebrows shooting up. "Pardon?"

"I met him at The Wicked Horse. It's just sex. There's nothing more than that to what we have."

Brandon frowns. "The Wicked Horse? What's that?"

I tell him exactly what it is. A sex club where people can indulge in their darkest desires. Brandon's face turns even redder. Now, doubt is written all over his face about me. I can see he's regretting handing Benjamin's address over.

I feel the need to explain. "I think he went there to feel something. And the connection you saw between us… I feel like I need to be truthful about it just being sexual in nature. But… it *was* a connection. I've never felt it before. You said you saw it, and I know it was real. We had something, but I don't know what it was."

The internal conflict within Brandon is apparent on his expression. It's clear he must've believed we had some sort of emotional bond, and I've just disabused him by clarifying it was sexual only. I think it might put me back in the category of a potential crazy stalker.

Which is why his next words surprise me greatly. "He wasn't always a dick. Before the accident, he was a good man. Happy, funny, caring, inclusive. He loved his patients. Had an incredibly close relationship with his parents and his brother. He was my best friend. There isn't anything he wouldn't tell me. I would love to see him get back there. And whether all you had between you was sex, maybe you are the person to get him there."

Shaking my head, I take a step backward. "Oh, I don't think so. It's not about that. I just wanted to make sure he's okay."

"Go see him," he instructs. "Make sure he's okay. And if something comes of it… great. If not, well, at least you'll know."

It hurts my heart to hear her how morose Brandon's tone is, which tells me he really doesn't garner much hope that I'm truly the one to bring Benjamin back. He's grasping at straws.

But I give Brandon a nod before tucking the address in my back pocket. It's the least I can do.

CHAPTER 17

Benjamin

THE TWO BOTTLES of liquor tucked into a brown paper bag setting on my front passenger seat clink together as I take a right-hand turn onto the street where I live. When I left my house half an hour ago, my intention was to run to the grocery store for some food. I made it as far as the liquor store, deciding to drink my dinner instead. This is surprising given the copious amounts of alcohol I drank last night.

Apparently, getting drunk was exactly what I needed. By the time I stumbled out of the club and into an Uber to take me home, I wasn't thinking about Cassidy, April, Elena, or anything else. It was a quiet, drunken bliss inside my head.

I don't have any surgeries scheduled tomorrow so I have no qualms with getting stupid drunk again tonight. I suspect this is more to keep thoughts of Elena away at this point since I have successfully made it past Father's Day, but whatever.

Thank fuck Elena wasn't at The Wicked Horse last night. Jerico surprised me with his personal knowledge of her schedule of attendance at his sex club. She never went on Sundays because she spent that day with her family. And why wouldn't she? Elena is incredibly family oriented. Another reason we don't belong together.

I'm not sure what I would have done had she shown up last night. Would I have stood by and watched her fuck someone else? I had no right to deny her. Yet, I feel like I might have made a scene. Not from the alcohol... but from something deep inside me that still believes she's mine. Inherently, I know I would flip out if another man even looked at her, much less touched her.

Sadly, it's not an acceptable way to feel—nor is it fair.

That means I need to stay away from the club. She still has a couple of weeks left on the thirty-day membership I got her. My plan is to stay out of there until her membership expires, and I hope to hell I never run into her there again.

Well, that's not exactly true. Every part of my being wants to run into her again. Be with her again. Be inside of her again.

Over and over again.

But the cost is way too high. The vulnerability and the way she strips me bare comes with too much risk of pain. It does too much to make me remember the loss I've already suffered, and I don't even want to consider a loss that could occur if I got tied in deep with her.

These thoughts preoccupy me so much it barely penetrates there's a car in my driveway as I slow on approach. It's a nondescript charcoal-gray car I immediately recognize as Elena's. At the end of every evening with her at the club, I'd escorted her back to that same vehicle.

One night, as I'd been kissing her goodbye, it had turned hot and heavy between us. I'd ended up hiking up her skirt, bending her over the hood, and fucking her hard from behind. Luckily, only one other couple had walked by us during our interlude. They'd been club members, so it hadn't been awkward in the slightest as they moved past us, even with their eyes glued to our straining bodies.

The thought of that night—boldly taking what I wanted without a care in the world—makes my dick twitch. Regrettably, it only gets more interested as she steps out of the car. It quickly lengthens behind the zipper of my pants, my breath turning ragged as I take her in.

I maneuver my car in beside hers, letting my gaze rake her over without shame. She's incredibly beautiful in just a pair of jeans with rips across the thighs and an off-the-shoulder white blouse. With her hair in a ponytail, she looks fresh and innocent.

Why is she here? How does she even know where I live?

And why in the fuck is there a feeling of joy bubbling up inside me when I have firmly decided, without equivocation, that she is simply no good for me?

It's with resolve I exit my vehicle and move around the front so I can meet her head-on.

"I'm sorry for just showing up," she rushes to say as we come face to face, her expression wary and slightly fearful even.

Oddly, I don't even have an ounce of anger she could be some weirdo stalking me. However, my curiosity shines through. "How did you find out where I live?"

I mean, it wouldn't be hard. Property tax records and all.

Which is why I'm surprised when she replies, "Your medical partner, Dr. Aimes. I went to your office today because I was worried about you. He told me where you live."

I'm going to fucking kill him. Not for the invasion of privacy, but for putting her back in my path. For tempting me with something I've already decided is no good.

Elena crosses her arms and tilts her chin up, giving me a harsh glare. "Why did you ghost me?"

I'm not prepared for her simple question. I'd expected it to be recriminations first, but it appears she just wants a straightforward answer.

"I'm sorry," I say sincerely. "I should have canceled."

Fire flashes in her eyes, and her jaw locks. "Explain,"

she corrects with an icy look. "You should've explained."

"It's complicated," I say, painfully aware of how lame my excuse is.

Elena throws her arms out, her voice heavy with sarcasm. "Yeah, I figured out you're a complicated guy. Knew it from the get-go, Benjamin. That's not really an excuse."

"I don't know what to say." She's right, of course. There was no good excuse for standing her up. But if I am going to hold true to the life I've been living since the accident, I don't owe her an explanation.

It's over. She should've taken the hint.

Regardless, I feel like I need to offer another apology. "I'm terribly sorry. But it's just not going to work, and I hope you can accept that."

I start to move past her, realizing my precious liquor is still in the front seat of my car, but I need to get away from her right now more than I need to start drinking.

"I know about your wife and daughter," she says, and I freeze in place.

Pain lances through me, and I'm paralyzed. My throat moves, but no sound comes out. I can't even turn to face her.

"And I'm so terribly sorry, Benjamin." I don't hear her move, but I sense her right behind me, then feel her soft hand on my back. "I can't even imagine going through what you did or what it must feel like."

I welcome the flush of anger her words cause, and I

wheel around on her. "And you what? Thought it might explain my motivations?"

She's not cowed in the slightest. Merely lifts her chin a little higher. "Does it?"

Another flash of fury moves through me, white-hot now with the need to make her understand me. My hand flies out to snatch her by the wrist. I turn to my front door, then drag her along behind me. "Come with me."

I haul her right up to my house, not slowing my pace even though she has to run to stay in stride with me. After I unlock the door, I pull her in behind me, releasing my hold once we're inside.

"Look," I order, sweeping my hand toward the interior of my home.

Her gaze moves around my living room, taking in the gloom and the covered furniture. The bare walls. The empty shelves. The darkened kitchen with nothing on the counters.

I put my hand on her back, then push her through my house down the hallway where I point to a closed door. "That's my daughter's room. I haven't even opened the door since I came home from the hospital."

She makes a small sound of distress, but I ignore it, propelling her farther along. I point to the master bedroom. "That's the room I shared with April. Been in there a few times, mostly just to move my stuff out."

I glide my hand up her back, curl around her neck, and physically turn her to the guest bedroom. Throwing the door open, I point inside. "This is my existence now. It's simple. Within these walls, I don't dwell on my past."

I hope my answer makes everything clear. It should be fucking clear. I am a man without anything important in my life. I don't need anything past what I have right now.

I turn slightly, dip my head, and take her in. Her face is strangely blank, as if she doesn't understand anything I've just shown her.

She tilts her head. "But why did you cut me out? Nothing you've said or shown me explains that. We had a connection, Benjamin. I know we did. And we made that connection even though you're living this existence."

My anger dissipates almost immediately, and I give a rough, ragged sigh. Scrubbing my hand through my hair, I admit, "Yes, we did have a connection. I hadn't had one in a long time."

"Then why?" she demands. "Why did you just decide it was over?"

I shrug, not because I don't know the answer. I just don't want to admit my weaknesses. "Because it ran its course. There was nothing more to it."

I don't know if I should be amused when Elena actually stamps her foot and puts her hands on her hips while growling, "Bullshit. You said you don't dwell on your past, yet you live in this ghost house." I find I have to hide an unwanted smile at her show of temper, and it only pisses me off more.

"Don't you dare judge me," I growl.

"I don't," she retorts. "I pity you. If you could just take a step and move past your fears, you could be happy again."

There is no holding my roar of fury back. "I don't want to be happy again. Don't you get it? I don't deserve it. April and Cassidy don't have the chance at happiness, so why should I?"

Elena's face softens, and I hate the look of sympathy. "You're wrong about their happiness. They're both in heaven. Happy and peaceful. They're probably sad over what you're doing to yourself, though."

I can't help but sneer. "What do you know about it?"

Her expression is incredulous, as if my question is senseless.

"I go to church," she replies with quiet confidence. "I believe in God, and I have faith we're all rewarded after we die."

I give a dismissive wave of my hand. "It's a farce. There is no God. If there is, he's not the loving deity you all worship. He would never do what he did to my family if that were so."

"He would if you had a different purpose," she says softly, but her voice contains surety. "If they weren't your end goal. Maybe they had fulfilled their purpose. Maybe they deserved the light and peace and joy. This world is hard, Benjamin, as you well know. April and

Cassidy are not suffering anymore."

I've had enough. I don't need to hear this bullshit. Iciness filling me, I point down the hallway. "You need to go. I'm tired, and I have an early day tomorrow."

She takes one last stab at getting something from me. Her tone sounds desperate. "So that's it? You're not going to talk about it anymore?"

"You need to leave," I repeat.

It causes me true pain when I see sorrow flash through her eyes and a certain regret for ever having met me. In this moment, I realize I've truly hurt her, and I never wanted that.

"Do you mind if I use the remainder of the membership at The Wicked Horse?" she asks, and I don't detect a single shred of her seeking vengeance in that request. I don't think she's asking to get me to change my mind or hurt me, but rather as a means for her to move on.

My jaw locks, but I manage to grit out. "Of course I don't mind. Enjoy."

Her chin lifts, a clear indication she's resolved about accepting the end of our agreement. "I will. Thank you."

So polite. That's how it ends between us.

She turns around and walks down my hallway, then through the kitchen, into the living room, and out my front door.

CHAPTER 18

Elena

"**I**T'S A DUMB idea, Elena."

Jorie's words resound in my head even though she said them to me well over an hour ago. It was a short phone conversation where I'd told her I was headed to The Wicked Horse. In my mind, I could see her lips pursed in dismay and her head shaking slightly in admonition.

She doesn't like I'm using the sex club to get over Benjamin or that I feel the need to get over a man in such a way.

"You weren't anything to him, Elena, so why should he be so much to you?" she'd asked.

I wish I knew the answer to that. Wish I could explain how hurt I am he called things off between us.

The irony we fell victim to the same things we were both trying to avoid sits heavily in my stomach. We had both closed ourselves off to true intimacy. To us, sex was a release. It didn't involve feelings. It was why we'd gone to The Wicked Horse in the first place.

But we'd both been affected by the other. I suspect Benjamin ended up letting himself go, opening himself up to his feelings, then got scared from the sensation. I'd also opened up, slightly willing to start believing not all men were the same. While I was scared, I was still willing to push forward.

And therein lays the difference. Benjamin simply isn't willing to do the same.

And it hurts.

A lot.

The only way I know to move past him, rather than moping over him, is to get back in the saddle again.

Or... on a cock for a cruder perspective.

It's time for the old Elena to return, immersing herself in pleasures of the flesh and locking her heart away tight once again.

Even though Jorie urged me to wait a few days, I don't understand what difference that would make. I won't feel any different tomorrow or the next day. I will continue to partake in the pleasures offered at The Wicked Horse as I have always done using the temporary membership she'd bought for my birthday. In my mind, there is no solid reason to wait.

Yes, I'm going to fuck Benjamin right out of my existence. And I don't have a single qualm about it. It's not like it would hurt him. He's the one who broke things off.

He'd said we had run our course, so it was time for me to chart a new one.

I strut through the club, confident in the way I look. After I left Benjamin's house and he had given me full permission to use the club, I went shopping and splurged on a sexy new dress. I then went home and pampered myself all afternoon by taking a luxurious bath and giving myself a pedicure and manicure.

Taking my time, I styled my hair in gorgeous, sexy waves, then expertly applied my makeup to accentuate my eyes, cheekbones, and lips.

I'm a fucking knockout and I know it, hence the reason for the strut.

The dress I bought is mint green with a slight silver shimmer throughout. It has a low-cut halter top and a form-fitting bodice, and it drops to just below my ass cheeks. A pair of four-inch silver sandals complete my ensemble. I'm going to get laid well tonight. There's no doubt about it.

I make my way to The Silo, refusing to give in to the small twinge of guilt simmering low in my belly. The Silo had been my choice because it's where I get the most worked up, and I know it won't take me long to find someone in there. The Silo is not about sensuality or slow arousal. Rather, it caters to those who like hardcore, fast fucking and dirty kink. I shove the kernel of guilt down even farther because it's unfair Benjamin can make me feel this way. I resent it. We don't owe each other anything at this point. No loyalty, no dues. Certainly no more care, concern, desire, or lust.

Tonight, I'm going to purge him from my system—hopefully with multiple amazing orgasms.

For a Monday night, it's crowded in The Silo. So many beautiful men and women to play with. So many toys to use. Jorie's brother, Micah, makes some of the sex toys showcased in here, which goes to show there are many things people can do with an engineering degree.

As I wind my way through the crowd, I nod at several people I know. There's an oval bar in the middle of the room, and I take a seat on the far side so I can watch the action in the glassed-in rooms. When I plop my butt on the seat, my skirt rides up so high half my ass hangs out, but it doesn't make me feel self-conscious. If anything, having my body on display makes me feel even sexier, as does knowing someone will want me tonight.

I order a dirty martini, letting my eyes roam around the room. There are a few men I've been with over the past few years here. If I want, there are solid repeat potentials available. It would cut out any small talk. The man across the bar has a solid knack for hitting my G-spot with his fingers, creating an orgasm unlike any other.

That could be nice tonight.

I move my gaze beyond him, latching on to two men entering the room.

They're both tall and intensely good looking, and I

realize I know one of them.

August Greenfield.

He works for a company called Jameson Force Security, which is owned by a man named Kynan McGrath.

Kynan is a former member of this club who I'd been with once before and it was a "once" I'll never forget. Kynan was well known by many of the ladies and even some of the men because he's adventurous and pretty much spent all his free time here. But he's now firmly off the market, engaged to actress and singer Joslyn Meyers. They both now live in Pittsburgh where he moved to open up a new headquarters for Jameson Force Security.

August locks eyes on me. He and I have exchanged flirtations—a.k.a. dirty talking—but we've never done anything. Not from lack of desire, but rather from no opportunity. Each time we've met up, one of us had already made solid plans with somebody else.

His gaze runs over my body, and it's obvious he likes my dress. When he nudges the man with him, they both move my way.

August has brown hair with a reddish tint and brilliant green eyes. He's tall and lanky, but the sexiest thing about him by far is his mouth. His lips are full, and he has a set of sexy dimples that always seem to be pitted with amusement. He's devilishly handsome with a confidence that only lends to his attractiveness.

The man with him is just as tall, but he's built twice as wide. He has on a pair of dark gray dress slacks and a formfitting black button-down shirt that seems to have been custom made to fit over his bulging muscles. He's got raven-black hair and crystal blue eyes that seem to penetrate straight through me.

As the men approach, I swivel my stool toward them, uncrossing my legs before crossing them again. As one, their eyes drop to get a peek. If they'd been quick enough, they now know I'm not wearing any panties.

"Elena," August says in a gruff, appreciative voice. Leaning down, he brushes his lips across my cheek. "Please tell me I've found you on a night when you don't have any plans."

My laugh is husky, but it carries a slight tinge of nervousness. It appears I'm going to be getting laid sooner rather than later, and I push that guilty feeling away.

"I just got here, and I've barely taken a sip of my martini," I say vaguely, but I give him a wide smile to convey interest. I don't know what my hesitation is in committing to him, because I know he would be an excellent lover. I've watched him fuck other women on occasion, and they had clearly enjoyed it if their moans and blissed-out expressions were any indication.

August makes a sweeping motion toward the dark-haired man. "This is my teammate, Cage Murdock."

When I hold my hand out, he takes it, pulling my knuckles to his lips.

"So you work for Kynan as well?" I ask.

Cage gives a nod. "Sure do. I'm based out of the new Pittsburgh headquarters but I'm in town for a few days and thought I'd visit my favorite place here." My gaze goes to August. "And you?"

"I like it fine right here in Vegas." His eyes roam over me, settling on my breasts for a moment before coming back to meet mine. He gives me an impish grin. "The scenery is fantastic."

Cage and August order drinks. We make small talk and flirt, laying down enough sexual innuendo there's no doubt how this evening is going to end.

When I get near the bottom of my martini, August asks, "Would you like another?"

I shake my head. "I usually only drink one. I don't like my senses to be dulled."

He nods, touches my arm with the back of a knuckle, then runs it lightly over my skin, causing me to shiver. "Just how adventurous are you, Elena?"

My mouth goes dry, but I manage to reply, "Very. What did you have in mind?"

August cuts a look toward his buddy, then gives his attention back to me. "Are you interested in taking us both on at the same time?"

While I've done a lot of dirty stuff in the sex club, I've never been with two men at the same time. I've been fucked by more than one man in the same evening, but I've never had two inside my body at once. I'm not going to lie—I get wet thinking about it. There's not a shred of guilt anymore. It's been fully replaced with burning lust.

"I think I would like to give it a try," I murmur. My intention isn't to come off coy, but it does just the same.

"Anal?" August asks for clarity. "Can you take my cock there?"

My mouth goes even drier. I lick at my lips, giving a short nod.

"Both of us at the same time?" he pushes, making sure we are clear on my boundaries. "Cage will take your pussy while I take your ass."

I start to agree, but something in the corner of my eye catches my attention. Shocked, I whip around, my brows shooting up when Benjamin steps up beside me. He's glaring with a ferocity I've never seen before, and it's directed at August and Cage.

He only gives them a moment before his hot eyes land on me. In a clipped tone, he snaps, "Elena."

"Benjamin," I reply curtly, then start to turn away from him.

But his words stop me cold. "You didn't waste much time."

It's an uncalled-for accusation, and I whirl on my seat to face him. "You didn't wait long either."

With nothing but a blasé shrug, Benjamin orders a bourbon from the approaching bartender. I continue to glare at him, but he ignores me.

So be it.

With as much dignity as I can muster, I rise to grab

August and Cage by their hands. "Let's go get a room."

"Would you like to invite your friend to come with us?" August asks. The question isn't issued in a polite way. Instead, it clearly spells out he hadn't liked the tone Benjamin addressed me with. August uses his words to rub Benjamin's nose in the fact I'm choosing to go with August and Cage.

Benjamin stares stonily across the room, pointedly ignoring us, but I don't spare him more than a glance.

"No thank you. I believe the two of you are more than enough to satisfy me."

I swear I hear a growl from deep within Benjamin, but I don't acknowledge it as I lead August and Cage away from the bar toward a hallway running along the perimeter of The Silo. From there, we can go into one of the empty glassed-in rooms to fuck on full display for everyone to see.

My heart beats wildly out of control, but it has nothing to do with the fact I'm soon going to let two men inside my body at the same time. Instead, it has everything to do with Benjamin being there to see me.

Clearly, though, he doesn't give a shit, which hurts more than it should. I wish it would make me want to put on a show just to spite him. Instead, it's only causing me to have major doubts.

As soon as we are in the room with the door closes behind us, August makes his move. He steps up to me, frames my face with his hands, and gives me a deep, searing kiss. Trying to relax, I force myself to melt into his embrace.

Cage comes up behind me, his hands going to my hips. The material of my dress starts to snake upward, and cool air hits my ass.

His mouth goes to my neck where he gives a not-so-subtle bite, one of his hands dropping between my legs.

Suddenly, the door flies open. While Cage and August do nothing but flick lazy, nonchalant glances that way, I jolt as if a lightning bolt has speared through me.

Standing in the doorway, looking like an enraged bull, is Benjamin. His face is red, his eyes are rolling, and his fists are clutched to the knob on the end of his cane so hard his knuckles are white. He may not have the military experience these two men do, but right now, I get the distinct impression he could take them both with the strength of his fury.

"Get your fucking hands off her right now," he snarls at the two men caging me in.

Neither man moves. Benjamin steps into the room, then lifts his cane a few inches from the floor before tossing it up about a foot. His hand strikes fast, grabbing it at mid-shaft. With that move, it became a weapon.

I don't know August well—Cage at all—but if they're even anything like the other people I know who work for Jameson Force Security, they are usually Special Forces with a healthy dose of alpha-male confidence. I would not expect them to give up the woman standing between them very easily.

"Elena," August says in a low, calm voice. "What do you want us to do?"

What do I want? Well, I don't want Benjamin to go down for assault. I have no doubt he'd start cracking heads if they don't move away from me.

"If you don't mind," I reply evenly, never taking my eyes off Benjamin, "I think I'll take a rain check with you and Cage."

Benjamin growls and takes a step toward us, rage I'd even suggest rescheduling the threesome flashing in his eyes.

Quickly, I amend, "Actually, I think we're just going to have to cancel permanently."

At this point, I'm not saying it to save August and Cage's hides, but rather... because I only want Benjamin. Relief fills me at his presence—at his caveman-like attitude as he claims me.

I'm still so stunned at his interruption, at his anger at what I was about to do, that I barely even comprehend what he's doing as he pulls me into his arms. His hand goes to the nape of my neck and he grips a handful of my hair, pulling on it roughly to tip my head up to meet his eyes.

"Nobody fucks you but me," he murmurs so possessively a tremor shoots up my spine, my legs pressing together to alleviate the surge of lust building there.

Helplessly, I keep my gaze pinned on his, only vaguely sensing August and Cage moving toward the door.

"Don't," Benjamin orders, and I'm confused about what he means. Is he talking to me?

But then he swivels his head to pin his gaze on Cage and August.

"Stay and watch. It will be worth it… I promise."

I drag my eyes from Benjamin to the two men, and I see lustful interest in their expressions. Hope they'll maybe get a taste.

Benjamin quickly disabuses them. "You aren't touching her, though."

CHAPTER 19

Benjamin

I AM OFFICIALLY fucked in the head. I'm so furious with Elena for wanting to fuck those two men, and yet at the same time, I'm also turned on by the fact she had *wanted* to fuck two men. Had *wanted* to take both at once.

How the fuck can I be turned on by that, yet want to kill the men who had dared to touch her?

Worst of all, why am I even doing this? I'd already cut her loose. I'd determined it was in my best interest, but I'd never felt such relief as I had when she chose me over them.

Elena stares up with soft brown eyes, trusting she's right where she needs to be. I hate that for her, because I have no clue what I can offer her for a future. Probably nothing outside the walls of this sex club, and I'm a selfish fuck for claiming this.

The door to our room opens, then closes with a soft noise. I assume those two assholes left, but I don't give a shit. The offer for them to stay and watch had been genuine, but it was more for my benefit than theirs. I wanted them to see what they'd never have.

Elena strains against my grip so she can look that way, but when a growl rumbles deep in my chest she swivels back toward me. My hold on her hair relaxes minutely when she freezes.

"What in the fuck am I doing?" I rasp, hoping to hell she's got an answer for me because I'm totally lost.

"Apparently, you are claiming what's already yours." Her voice is husky with desire, and it's exactly what I need to hear. I'd been afraid she would say something too intimate like "following your heart" or "seeking happiness". I would've bucked against any response like that. Possibly even walked out the door.

Oh, who the fuck am I kidding... I can't walk away from her.

I'm also not sure if I can give her much more than orgasms, either.

But great sex is going to have to be enough.

Dipping my head, I bring my mouth to hers. She gasps, and I can tell it's because she was expecting a full onslaught given the fact I'm still buzzing with an anger-fueled energy.

But miraculously, my kiss is sensuously soft—gentle even—as I graze my lips ever so slowly against hers.

Her breath flutters out in a sigh as her arms wrap around my neck. She leans her body into mine, but not in a sexual way. Not even in a submissive way. Instead, it feels like support.

Not that lust is absent. It's coursing through me like a wildfire, and my cock is hard as granite.

But for right now, it's enough that Elena—in this moment—is mine.

The cane slips from my fingertips, clattering to the wood floor. After working the knot of her halter-top dress free, I slowly pull it down past her breasts. Slip my thumbs into the edge of the material and push it down her body, squatting as I go. When it moves over her hips, I realize she has no panties on. I can't help but pause. Press my lips to her smooth pussy before she gracefully steps out of her dress. I ignore her sexy-as-fuck sandals, choosing to let her keep those on as they'll look beautiful propped on my shoulders.

I straighten, kiss Elena again, and move her toward the bed without breaking the contact. We're in The Silo, the dirtiest, kinkiest sub-room of The Wicked Horse, yet I have no desire to use any of the sensual props that are widely stocked throughout.

All I want is Elena in her purest form, her beautiful body bare and available to my hands, mouth, body, and cock.

Her legs hit the bed, and I lower her down. She never takes her eyes off me, and I only know this because I can't take mine off her.

I release my hold on her, straighten once again, and

start to remove my clothes. She watches me with keen eyes as I strip layer after layer off my body until I'm completely naked and I've got my hardened cock in my hand stroking it.

She seems in a daze for a moment. But when I take a step toward the bed, she moves hastily backward, making room for me.

Her arms come up as she reaches out for me.

One knee to the mattress, a hand by her ribs, and the other to Elena's face, I cover her body with mine. Her legs spread and wrap around me. My cock instinctively finds her warmth. My hips move as my mouth takes hers again in yet another slow, deep, and consuming kiss. I slide in deep, her wetness a testament to what she feels for me.

A fucking divine validation of how much she wants me.

"Benjamin," she gasps into my mouth as I hit deep and press hard against her. Christ, that feels way too good.

But I knew it would.

Every time with Elena, it just feels too fucking good. It's why she's dangerous. It's also why I apparently can't let her go.

There on silken sheets with our mouths fused together, one of her hands tangled in my hair and one of mine holding tightly onto her hip, I fuck her slowly and without a timetable to release. There's no rush. No people outside the glass with their greedy, lustful eyes on us. I have nowhere else I'd rather be than in this moment of pleasure and sensation.

Knowing deep in my gut even if I'm too fearful to admit it, I might be a little too lost in Elena. There's a very real chance I'm setting myself up to experience pain again by giving in to this need to be with her.

◆

IT'S PART OF the unwritten club rules that after members have finished fucking in one of the rooms, they are to vacate sooner rather than later. This lets discreet workers come in, clean the place up, and ready it for the next hedonists to enter.

We've overstayed our limit for sure, yet I don't want to pull away from Elena. I came harder than I ever remember having done before. If the ferocity of her scream when she released is any indication, she's feeling as mellow as I am right now. I'm still on top of her, my cock having already softened and slipped out of her heat. Her hands lazily stroke my back. While I hold most of my weight off her with my forearms into the mattress, my head lays heavy on her breasts.

"Benjamin," Elena whispers, and I feel her head turn so her lips press briefly to the top of my head. "We should probably get going."

I lift my head so I can see her. Her expression is soft and satisfied. She looks wrecked, and I love being the one to have caused it.

It's been a long fucking time since I've taken such immense pride in what I can do to a woman.

My dick pulses at the thought of doing it again. I lean down and kiss Elena. Her tongue touches mine without hesitation, and I start to swell. Christ, I want her again.

I pull my mouth from hers with a sigh, wondering just how ensnared I've become by this woman. My head tilts, and I look out the glass wall to see those two men who were in here with her standing there…. watching. One of them smirks in a knowing way as if to say, "Yeah, buddy… you are so fucking whipped right now."

Asshole.

Part of me wants to show him differently. Show them both.

My eyes cut to one of the sex toy machines in the corner. It's a contraption that has a jackhammering dildo a woman crouches over. I could put Elena on it, let it take her from below while I fuck her ass.

It would show them there's nothing they can give her that I can't do better.

Except… is that better?

Does she want the experience of two men?

Do I have the capability to give her that? The thought of another man touching her makes me want to kill, but… could I put that aside for her?

I'm not sure, but now it's going to gnaw at me until I

know for sure.

I look back to Elena, whose eyes are still on my face while her fingers play in my hair.

"Do you want to be with more than one man at the same time?" I ask bluntly.

She blinks in surprise. "Um…"

"Because if you do—"

"Actually no," she says so quietly I barely hear her, yet I'm immensely relieved when I make the words out.

"Are you sure?" I press.

She shrugs. "I mean… I was curious about it. And that's why you and I come to The Wicked Horse, right? For that type of debauchery? And well, you and I weren't together anymore, and they offered, so…"

"I'll make it happen for you if you want," I say, my gut churning over my rash offer. But strangely, I find myself wanting to offer her the moon if I could, which I can't. So I offer her something else instead.

She shakes her head, bringing a hand to my jaw where she caresses it. "I'm going to say something at the risk of freaking you out, but honestly Benjamin… when I'm with you, I don't need anything else. Not another man or two other men—not the toys here at the club. And I'm not saying it in a possessive way. Nor am I declaring my devotion to you or expecting anything from you in return. I'm merely saying you completely satisfy me sexually. There's nothing else I need."

I can't help but smile as I bend, bringing my face

closer. "Jesus… now I want to fuck you again."

She grins back. "I would not say no to that."

I had forgotten my earlier vision of her silver sandals propped on my shoulders, having been too lost inside of her previously. I rear up, push my palms under her thighs, and raise her legs high in the air. Tilting my hips, I'm able to align myself easily. With one hard thrust, I'm deep into nirvana again.

Elena groans as I lean into her, pressing my palms into the mattress. Her calves come to rest on my shoulders, causing her to fold almost in half as I start to fuck her again.

This time, it's not so slow.

It's a hell of a lot deeper with this angle.

Even better than the last time.

CHAPTER 20

Elena

"JUST CUT IT all off," Jorie says in frustration as she blows her bangs off her forehead. She's my last customer of the day, which on a Saturday would normally be a five PM appointment, but I'm actually going on a date with Benjamin, so I scheduled her for three. When we're done, I'm closing shop.

"Are you sure?" I ask as I stand behind her chair, working the pedal at the bottom to pump her up a little higher.

My gaze watches her through the mirror as she studies her raven-black hair. She had been wearing it in a short, angular bob with her bangs cut sharply straight across her brow, which did wonders for her sea-green eyes. But she's been trying to grow it out lately, more from being so busy she didn't have time to drive out to me in Henderson to get it cut.

Jorie holds a chunk of her hair near her temple outward, studying it critically in the mirror. "Would it be stupid for me to cut it all off?"

"Well, define what you mean by 'cut it all off,'" I say. "Are we talking a get-the-electric-razor Sinead O'Connor cut or maybe a Ginnifer Goodwin pixie?"

"Totally Ginnifer Goodwin—from *Once Upon a Time*," she says with a lopsided grin, referencing our favorite TV show. Too bad the final season was so awful.

When I shoot her a dreamy smile in return, we sigh and say at the exact same time, "Mmm... Captain Hook."

I snort, and she giggles as I run my fingers through her hair. "Will Walsh care if you cut it off?"

"Pfft." She rolls her eyes. "I don't care if he cares. It's my hair, but I doubt he would. He's totally seen me at my worse, and he still seems to love me."

My mind drifts to Benjamin and our rendezvous last night at The Wicked Horse. He had me on the see-through floor of The Deck—which is forty-plus stories above the streets of Vegas—and he'd fucked my brains out from behind. He'd wrapped the length of my hair around his hand and wrist. Forced my head backward to stare at the stars. I came so hard I'd seen double.

After we'd finished, he'd gently released my hair from his grip and muttered, "Love this fucking hair of yours."

The words had been said gruffly, but they'd held such affection my heart tripped over. Benjamin is usually anything but affectionate, but he is a great fuck, so at least there's that… even if his tone had confused me.

"I know that look on your face," Jorie says slyly, throwing me a wink through the mirror. "Might as well spill it all and update me."

"Make a decision on your hair first," I demand. "I can talk while I cut."

"Ginnifer Goodwin me up," she replies adamantly.

I give her a poke in the ribs. "Okay… sit up straight, though."

Grumbling, she straightens her spine. "Don't you need to wash my hair first?"

"Nope," I say as I reach into the top drawer of my station to pull out my folding razor, then flourish it above her head with a grin. "Going old school."

"Cool," she replies.

Picking up a lock of her hair, I start sawing away. I make chunky cuts I'll feather more delicately later, but I brace myself for more questions.

"So, spill everything about Benjamin."

Jorie knows we've reconnected. I called her the morning after he showed up at The Wicked Horse and stopped my planned threesome. When I'd explained how Benjamin stormed in, brandished his cane threateningly, and ran the two alpha dudes off—as well as how totally hot it made me—and that we'd had the most amazing sex ever and were seeing each other again, Jorie had agreed it was sexy, but she'd been surprisingly close-mouthed with her opinions.

"What does it mean?" was all she'd asked.

When I'd had to reply with, "I'm not really sure," Jorie had only hummed before changing the subject.

That was four nights ago.

I don't have any more clarity really, so I fill her in on the facts. "We've seen each other every night this week."

"All at The Wicked Horse?" she asks.

It bugs me he hasn't offered to come to Henderson like he had before we broke up, and it must show in my tone. "Yeah... all at The Wicked Horse."

Her expression is sharp. "Is that all it is then? Just club sex?"

"What else would it be?" I ask with a light laugh and a wave of my hand.

Appearing perplexed, she shrugs, but luckily not while I'm in the midst of cutting. "I don't know... I was hoping perhaps his display of jealousy meant something more."

"Well, it sort of did. I mean... he's made it clear he doesn't share."

"Big whoop," she mutters with an eye roll. "I want a magnificent display or a grand gesture or something."

"I'm not so sure I do," I say hesitantly.

"Bullshit," she snaps, and I stare at her through the mirror for a moment. "You were really hurt when he called things off. You have feelings. The mere fact you are monogamous rather than getting your rocks off with random dudes, which has been your modus operandi forever now, is telling."

I don't fall for her bait—just blow her off. "Whatever. Right now, I'm happy. I'm having the best sex of my life, I've finally found a man who isn't codependent on me, and he treats me like a queen between the sheets. Tell me why that shouldn't satisfy me?"

"Because you're built to love someone," she murmurs. "I want you to have love the way I do. I want you to get married and have kids so our kids can play together, and you're full of shit if you say you don't want those things."

"I do," I admit. "You've known me our whole lives, so you know I do. I'm tired of always picking the losers who would make shitty husbands and even shittier fathers. It's easier to keep my expectations really low."

"So Benjamin is different in he's not relying on you to make him happy or support him, yet he's only good enough to see inside a sex club?"

Her question is disturbing because it forces me to face an ugly truth. I stop sawing on a lock of her hair, gazing at her through the mirror. "I think he's too broken to be a husband or a father again. And... he doesn't want me to fix him."

"But that's a good thing," Jorie points out.

"Yes, that's a good thing. What I should have said is he doesn't want to be fixed. So this is going to be nothing more than amazing sex, which will eventually run its course."

"I'm going to call bullshit again," Jorie demurs. "He made a claim on you. He's established a monogamous relationship with you. He wants something, that's for sure."

Could that be true? I don't want to get my hopes up. I saw how easy it was for Benjamin to just give up on things, and I'm still not sure why he broke things off to begin with. We haven't really talked about it.

Sure, we've fallen back into the same pattern where we'd meet up for drinks at The Wicked Horse before finding a room to fuck in, but our talks haven't been deep or consequential. It's clear we're both afraid to push too deep.

Besides, we communicate best when our clothes are off and we're immersed in each other.

Still, I play devil's advocate, running though scenarios where he does want me. As they play through my mind, I admit my darkest fear to Jorie. "I don't want to be the one who has to fix him, though. That never works out."

"Agreed," Jorie replies, twisting to see me. She even takes my free hand in hers, giving it a squeeze. "So sit back, relax, and enjoy the ride. Let things develop if they do. If they don't, at least you'll have no regrets for trying."

"Sounds simple enough," I say on a half-laugh, giving her hand a squeeze before I release it. I move my concentration to her hair, taking another piece and giving it a quick lop.

"Are you seeing him tonight?" Jorie asks.

My belly flutters as I pick up another piece of hair, setting the edge of the razor to it. "Yeah… actually, he asked me out to dinner."

"What?" she exclaims, turning quickly to look at me. My razor slices cleanly through her hair, luckily not taking off more than I'd intended.

"Jorie," I snap with irritation. "You could have caused me to cut down into your scalp or even taken off a finger of mine. Hold still, damn it."

She ignores me, eyes blinking rapidly in surprise. "Dinner? Like a date outside the club?"

"I guess," I reply hesitantly. "Although, I'm not quite sure. He asked me to meet him at the hospital as he's on call today."

"That's huge," she murmurs in awe.

"Not really," I reply, putting my fingertips to her jaw and forcing her around. "Now stay still."

I go to work again, cutting it to pixie length. Jorie watches me quietly, but I can tell she's gearing up to saying something important.

I start feathering the razor at her left temple, alternately running my comb through the pieces to critique the length and how they lay. Jorie's got the perfect face for this cut, and I wonder why I've never suggested it before.

"I'm worried now," she finally says, which surprises

me. I stop, look at her through the mirror, and tilt my head in question.

"Why's that?" I ask.

"Because, well... the way you've been painting things, I thought for sure this wouldn't go anywhere. But dinner is a pretty big deal for a man such as Benjamin."

"Yes, I could see that," I drawl hesitantly. "But I don't understand why that's concerning to you."

"Because... he really is a broken person, Elena. What he suffered...what he lost... do you really want to deal with that?"

I'm so shocked by the fear I hear in her tone that I walk around the chair so I can look at her face to face. She's now freaking me out a little. "What's really bothering you, Jorie? It's not like you to be wary of people because of their past. You're way too empathetic for that. You're the type of person who would bend over backward to help Benjamin overcome his past."

Her eyes drop a moment, cheeks turning slightly pink. I'm on to something. She's not being transparent with me.

"Jorie," I prompt. "What's really bugging you about Benjamin?"

She finally looks back up, swallowing hard before lifting her chin a bit defiantly. "You won't be his first love. You'll be second. You'll come after a wife and a daughter who will most likely always be above you, and you'll never live up to them in his eyes. And I see that as nothing but heartbreak and misery for you. I changed my mind about all of this. I don't want you to see him anymore. He's not good enough."

I'm completely blown away by her worries—about things I had never even considered. I was so worried about the basics with Benjamin... like having a genuine conversation or seeing a movie together at some point, I never considered what would happen if this turned into a real relationship.

And she has a very valid point.

How could I ever compete with a dead wife and child? It seems almost insurmountable.

"Call and cancel the date," she suggests quickly.

I'm shaking my head without any thought, going on gut instinct. "I don't want to."

"Oh, God," she moans over-dramatically. "You've already fallen for him, haven't you? You're already in too deep. Your heart's already in danger of being shattered by him."

"Jorie," I exclaim, partly in annoyance but partly in amusement. "Stop with the paranoia and hysteria. I'm going into this with my eyes open wide, and I'm not in danger of anything right this moment."

She just stares dubiously.

"Granted," I admit with an acknowledging incline of my head, "you've made some good points about where I might stand in the hierarchy of things with Benjamin, but we are nowhere near worrying about that just yet. It's still just sex, and I'm sure dinner probably has everything to do with the fact he's getting off call and will be hungry. I'm sure things are going to be fine."

But even as I say those words, I have to admit... she has me thinking. Should I even bother with a man who could potentially never be enough for me, because I am most likely never going to be enough for him based on what he used to have?

CHAPTER 21

Benjamin

I 'VE SEEN ELENA in any number of sexy outfits at The Wicked Horse. She likes them tight, short, and revealing, and I like them as well.

Like her better naked.

And yet, as I walk toward her in the lobby of the hospital's main floor, I don't know if I've ever seen her look more beautiful. I had merely told her I was taking her to dinner, then left it up to her what to wear because where I'm taking her, anything from jeans to a cocktail dress would be appropriate.

But she surprises me in a feminine wraparound dress in a floral print. It's ankle length in flowing layers. She has on a pair of nude-colored heels, and her makeup is very understated. Her hair is sleek and gathered at the nape of her neck. For jewelry, she has simple gold studs in her ears.

She looks amazing—completely out of character from the sex kitten I'd met and fucked at the club. I have to wonder which Elena is the real one. Perhaps she's a mixture of both.

"Hey," she says as I approach, her eyes taking me in. I dressed in jeans and a button-down shirt after my last surgery, opting for casual. I even put on tennis shoes rather than my standard loafers or the low boots I'd usually wear, but my leg is aching a bit after standing beside the operating table all day and comfortable shoes help.

"You look gorgeous," I say, noting her flash of surprise at my compliment as I bend in to brush my lips across her cheek.

"Thank you," she mumbles with a shy smile, and it's obvious she's completely off her game. Maybe the real Elena is the sex-club vixen who doesn't know how to be wooed.

Not that I'm trying to date her.

This probably isn't going to be what she'd been expecting when I said dinner, but where I'm taking her *is* a bit monumental.

I grab Elena's hand, position her on my non-cane side, then lead her out of the hospital. "Do you mind if we take my car?"

"Not at all," she replies.

We walk in silence across a small parking lot to a private lot for on-call doctors. I lead her over to my Audi Q8, open the door, and help her into the passenger seat. She's already buckled by the time I get in. Within moments, I'm pulling out of the hospital parking lot. I cross one intersection, turn right at the next, then pull into another parking lot. The entire journey takes less than a minute.

When I glance over at Elena, she's scanning our surroundings in surprise.

I pull up to the first four-story brick building, put the car in park, and then shut it off. She looks up at it for a moment before turning to me, curiosity burning in her eyes. "What are we doing here?"

"Dinner," I say with a smile before hopping out of the car. I move over to her door, open it, and help her out.

"At a friend's place?" she inquires as I lead her to the first-floor apartment directly in front of us.

"No," I say as I slip my key in the door. "My place."

I open the door, then let her step inside. She places her hand clutch on a small counter that separates the kitchen and living room, then examines my new but sparsely furnished apartment.

Pivoting, she faces me as I close the door. "This is your apartment?"

Nodding, I step past her, heading around the counter and into the kitchen. I place my cane up against the pantry door, comfortable without it in the kitchen since I can lean on counters if necessary. "Signed the lease two days ago. I'm still waiting on some furniture I ordered, and I don't have all my personal stuff moved over yet, but yeah… it's mine."

As I open the fridge and start pulling out stuff I'd pre-cut yesterday, Elena sits down at the small table that seats two. The apartment is small but luxuriously appointed. Hardwoods, crown molding, top-of-the-line fixtures, and appliances.

"Want some wine?" I ask.

"Sure," she replies, and I nab a bottle of red from a small wine rack that sits between fridge and sink. She watches me silently as I open the bottle, pulling out two wineglasses I'd bought and washed just yesterday. I didn't want to bring the ones I'd collected during my life with April. In fact, I'm starting over new with everything here.

I hand Elena a glass, then tap mine against hers. "Cheers."

"Cheers," she murmurs, but I can see she's incredibly confused.

Smiling over the rim of my glass, I move to take the other seat at the table. Dinner is a simple charcuterie board I'm going to put together along with a cobb salad, but that can wait.

"You said I was living in a ghost house," I say, and I'm charmed by the embarrassed flush to her cheeks.

"I shouldn't have said that," she mumbles apologetically. "I was awful."

"No," I correct. "You were truthful and absolutely right. And I was torturing myself there as well. I'm going to sell the house. There's no reason for me to stay there anymore, so I went ahead and rented this apartment that is convenient to the hospital until I can decide what I want to do permanently."

"Permanently?" she inquires before taking a sip of her wine.

"You know... whether I want to bother with home ownership or just stay in an apartment. Stay in the city or move to the burbs. Hell... potentially move to another city for all I know."

"Lots of choices," she murmurs, and I couldn't agree with her more. Suddenly, I realize I have a blank palette for my life now. I can paint whatever story I want.

I can't say Elena will be part of that story, but she did jar me enough to realize the life I was leading was too destructive for me. Ironically, she's the one who ultimately led to my freak-out last Friday, which caused me to back out of a surgery Brandon had to scramble to cover. Once I'd sobered up after Father's Day, it had hit me hard how fucked up my life was. I've been a dick, an asshole, and a virtually unlovable person over the past year, but I'd never let down a patient until then. Even though Brandon is as adept at performing the scheduled surgery as I am, it had been my patient. That meant they had put their trust in me, and I hadn't even fucking shown up.

I can't do that anymore.

I can't be that type of person.

And as long as I can have Elena on my terms, there's no reason I can't explore outside the walls I've erected, at least a little bit.

"Why are we here instead of the club?" Elena asks.

I'm caught completely off guard not only by her question, but also by the distrustful tone in her voice.

"Because I wanted to show you this place," I say truthfully. "And I thought we could perhaps continue what we have outside The Wicked Horse sometimes."

Her brows draw inward, knitting in consternation. "But this doesn't mean anything's changed between us, right? It's still just sex?"

"And dinner," I say with a quirk to my lips. "I mean… I'm pretty hungry and figured you are, too."

She just stares, and I don't know whether to be amused or offended. It's so strange for the woman to be the one suspicious of motivation. Moreover, for the woman to be so averse to a relationship. It's clearly why she's a little off-kilter tonight.

I reach out to take her hand, trying to reassure her. "Elena… I enjoy the hell out of fucking you. I've never been more compatible with a woman before—not like the way I am with you. You and I are so much alike in our desires to keep this casual, right?"

She nods slowly.

"So if you want, we'll only fuck at the club. But we can certainly fuck here, too, or even at your place sometimes. Just as long as we're clear on the boundaries, right?"

She nods again before taking another sip of wine. When she sets the glass down, her gaze hardens minutely. "But let's clarify a few things."

"Okay," I drawl hesitantly.

"I get this is just sex, and I'm fine with that. You're right… it's the only thing we're both interested in. But are we monogamous?"

"Yes," I answer firmly. I sure as fuck know a great thing when I see it—or rather, feel it—and I don't have interest in anyone else. In fact, I couldn't care less if we ever return to the club.

"Then I need you to explain something to me." Her voice dropped an octave, and I can tell this is important.

"What's that?"

"If sex is all this is, and all it will ever be, why did you break things off last time?" she asks. The hardnosed question causes my gut to pinch, because it means admitting a terrible vulnerability as well as divulging she's done a number on my head already.

I decide to tell her most of the truth. "I had not realized Father's Day was coming up. I'd overheard some people talking about it, and it caught me totally off guard. Frankly… I sort of spiraled down."

"That was the night you stood me up?"

I nod. "Stood you up. Canceled a surgery and sort of went off the grid for a few days. Drank a lot of alcohol."

"I'm sorry, Benjamin," she says. Her voice is so gentle, yet it's filled with hurt on my behalf. It makes my chest ache. "I hate that for you, and I can't even imagine what that was like."

My throat clogs with emotion, and I can't respond.

She squeezes my hand. "If you ever need a break again, I'll understand."

Fuck... the urge to cry from her understanding of my pain hits me hard. I can do nothing but give her a short squeeze back and a false smile, and I rise from my chair.

Giving her my back, I turn toward the fridge again to make our dinner. "I'm starved," I say lamely, grabbing the spring salad mix, tomatoes, cucumber, and an onion from the vegetable drawer. I move to the counter, keeping my back to her as I start to prattle on about my last surgery.

I let my hands work on our dinner while I use inane conversation to lead me away from the emotion that was starting to overwhelm me. Yet, I can't quite forget how much her empathy touched me.

Way too fucking deep.

I start to slice the cucumber when I feel her hand at my bicep. It slides down my arm, and I freeze into place. She takes the knife from me, sets it aside, and then curls her fingers around my bicep again whereby she gives a tug for me to face her.

I resist, terrified she'll want to talk things out with me or want to psychoanalyze my pain. I don't want to talk about it. Not with her. Not with the one person who has woken up the feeling within me in over a year.

"Benjamin," she calls gently.

Hesitantly, I turn to face her. When my eyes land on her, they widen in shock.

Elena is completely naked, and she has a playful smile on her face. All thoughts fly out of my head, and my cock responds accordingly.

And I can see by the expression on her face, it's exactly what she was aiming for. Elena was pulling me away from the emotion of the candid moment we shared, putting things back onto the only plane of existence that feels comfortable to me.

"We can eat later," she says.

I put my hands on her waist, and easily lift her to the counter that separates the kitchen and living room and is currently without vegetables and knives. Her legs spread and I step in between them, bringing my hands to her face so I can kiss the ever-loving fuck out of her. She puts her hands on my belt. While she works to free my cock, I thank my lucky stars I found a woman such as this.

One who knows my limitations and is fine working within them.

CHAPTER 22

Elena

I SLOWLY AWAKEN. The grayish light tells me that it's early morning, and I let a long, luxurious stretch overtake my body. My arms extend over my head, hands locking, and I reach out to touch the headboard—not the railing from my wrought-iron bed—and I realize I am not where I normally wake up on a Sunday morning.

My entire body locks tight. Slowly, I turn to the right and see I am all alone.

In Benjamin's bed.

I'm not sure whether to be disappointed or relieved. Disappointment would mean I remember the benefits of snuggling up to a man in the early morning hours after a long night of passionate lovemaking. There is something so comforting about pressing against a warm naked body, knowing it had cherished you the night before. But on the flipside, I should be relieved because Benjamin is most definitely not a snuggler and being rebuffed would be a cold slap in the face.

I decide I'm glad he's not a cuddler because it will be easier to keep him at arm's length.

I don't even recall falling asleep last night. We had some fast, amazing sex right on his kitchen counter. My goal had been to distract him from anything too serious, and sex had been the best way to do it. It hadn't been a hardship since I love everything about having sex with Benjamin. If I had to list my top three favorite hobbies, fucking Benjamin would currently be number one.

After that, we ate dinner at his little kitchen table. It was simple and delicious, and we'd paired it with a bottle of exceptional wine. Conversation had flowed without any real work on our part. That was probably because we skirted anything too deeply personal.

For example, we'd talked about career paths. I was incredibly curious as to what led him to become a doctor, and even more so a neurosurgeon. He'd wanted to know why I'd decided to be a business owner rather than work for someone else. That our careers and levels of income are so incredibly disparate hadn't entered the conversation, and it had pleasantly surprised me. It seems Benjamin doesn't care about the fact we're in different educational and socioeconomic classes. Then again, that might only be because there is nothing between us but sex. It's not like he has to take me to the country club or a high-powered medical conference where I would be forced to interact with people who are just not like me.

I never had any real belief the date would be over

after dinner, even though we'd already had sex. We usually went at it at least two times in an evening, sometimes three. As expected, Benjamin took control, which is what I love the most about him. He'd brought me into his bedroom, which he'd recently furnished with heavy masculine furniture, and we'd done an excellent job of breaking in his new mattress.

And there was nothing vanilla about it. We might not have been at The Wicked Horse, putting on a show for others, or using the abundance of implements and toys available, but we got dirty all the same. For the first time since we'd started sleeping together, Benjamin had claimed my ass. He'd done it after making effective use of a few of his silk ties. He'd tied one arm behind my back, then looped another tie around my head and mouth in a makeshift gag. After some incredible foreplay, which included him giving me two orgasms with his mouth, he put me on my knees, pressed my torso and cheek into the mattress, used his fingers and copious amounts of lube to prepare me, then took my darkest, tightest spot. When his broad cock had filled and stretched me, it had felt both incredible and painful at the same time. I'd loved every second of it.

I shiver, thinking about how he'd taunted me with dirty words. Mostly, he'd been asserting his claim on me. And now he owned every piece of me. He told me he'd wished he had taken my ass for the first time the night Cage and August were watching him, so they'd know exactly what they were missing.

I'd been pinned down by a strong hand in the middle of my back while he'd plundered my ass, yet I'd never felt so wanted, adored, and cared for in my entire life.

Afterward, I'd been wrecked. I remember him taking the ties off. After I flopped onto my stomach, Benjamin disappeared. He'd reappeared moments later with a warm soapy cloth and a towel. His gentleness as he'd cleaned me up had surprised me. When he'd left the second time, I must have fallen asleep.

I'm awake now, though, and the knowledge I'd breached one of the boundaries we'd set by spending the night in his bed rolls over me.

I scan the place Benjamin presumably slept. The covers are messed up, but that doesn't mean he spent the entire night beside me.

The pressure on my bladder urges me to put those thoughts aside, so I crawl out of bed. After using the bathroom just off the master bedroom, I slip my clothes on, grab my heels, and head into the kitchen.

I find Benjamin sitting at the little table, drinking a cup of coffee. Glancing at the clock on the wall, I note it's almost seven thirty. When my gaze lands on Benjamin again, I can't help musing over how incredibly beautiful and yummy he is in a pair of jeans and a white T-shirt, his feet bare. He's bent over his phone reading something, his other hand wrapped around a steaming mug of coffee. I study the fingers that have plundered parts of my body no one has ever touched, marveling at the fact they also perform delicate surgery on spines and brains. Capable in so many ways.

Even though I barely made a sound as I padded through his condo, he lifts his head as I approach. His smile is warm, which is reassuring. He could have greeted me with awkward tenseness over the fact we're forced to do the morning-after routine.

"Coffee?" he asks.

"Sure," I reply, scanning his kitchen. "I'll be glad to—"

Benjamin pushes up from the table, then points to the other chair. "Sit. I'll make it for you."

I take a seat as Benjamin moves over to a fancy-looking machine that appears to make coffee, espressos, and lattes.

"What's your poison in the morning?"

It's funny how I've submitted fully, given him my body, and entrusted him not to hurt me, but he has no clue what type of coffee I drink.

"Just a regular with a little bit of cream," I say.

He glances over his shoulder to give me a sheepish grin. "Sorry... No cream. Is black okay?"

"Of course," I reply, although I grimace on the inside. I hate black coffee, but I need caffeine.

Benjamin works the machine, which freshly grinds the beans, then brews a frothy cup. He returns, lowers into his own chair, then sets the cup on the table and nudges it toward me. "I'll pick up some cream for you at the grocery store today."

I hate that my heart flutters over such a simple offer. Again, it doesn't jive with the nature of the relationship we have set for ourselves. I want to hate myself for being charmed, but I also can't be overly surprised. Even though I'm okay with our emotionless, sex only relationship, I have to acknowledge how much I like this man and how I would potentially be open to more if he wanted it.

Picking up the cup, I blow on it slightly before taking a sip. It's surprisingly good, and I have to assume it's because he has a fancy coffee maker and expensive beans. Setting the cup back down on the table, I find him watching me.

I offer an apologetic smile. "I'm sorry I overstayed my welcome last night. You should have woken me up and pushed me out the door."

The expression on Benjamin's face doesn't give away anything, but I'm surprised when he says, "You didn't overstay your welcome. In fact, I'm glad you did. That way, I didn't worry about you driving all the way back to Henderson at night."

I don't even know what to say to that. Again, he seems to be pushing at the edges of the boundaries we had set.

"Breakfast?" he asks. "I can whip us up some eggs."

It would be entirely appropriate for me to raise an

eyebrow and ask, "Who are you and what have you done with Benjamin?"

Because it appears somebody new has inhabited his body this morning.

Instead, I shake my head with true regret. "I can't. I have to get going to meet my parents for church."

I am aware from our conversation at his house that Benjamin doesn't have much respect for the divine. Still, his tone is neutral when he asks, "Do you go every week?"

"I try to."

"Can I ask why?" He seems genuinely curious, but he can't hide the slight bit of derisiveness in his tone.

I pick my words carefully, keeping them truthful but light. "Lots of reasons. It reaffirms my faith, and it gives me comfort. I love the tradition and ceremony of the Catholic Church. I go with my family so we can spend time together and bond."

He stares, clearly considering my words.

And I can't help myself. "Have you ever been a churchgoer?"

It's the first question I have asked about his past that might cause some friction in our conversation. I have no clue why I'd decided to go there, but maybe it's because Benjamin has been pushing the boundaries we'd previously set. Perhaps I feel entitled.

To my surprise, he answers without any hesitation. "Growing up, I was. I would periodically go with April after we got married. But there always seemed to be too much to do on Sundays, particularly after we had Cassidy, that we sort of fell off. It was just never really important to me."

I'm absolutely stunned he offered the information up, even more so he would mention his late wife and daughter. If he were any other man, I'd engage in a friendly debate with him. Push him on his beliefs. But I remember all too clearly his disdain for God because Benjamin felt God was wrong to let that accident happen. While I would love to have enough of a bond with Benjamin to gently pursue this, it absolutely spells disaster. And I am not ready for him to cut me off again.

So I take a larger sip of coffee, set my cup back down, and then stand. "I really do need to get going. By the time I drive back to Henderson and get ready, I'll have to run out the door to make church."

Benjamin looks up from the table, then blinks a moment before standing as well. He looks a little bit lost as to what to do.

So I step into him, putting my hands on his waist and rising onto my tiptoes to give him a kiss. "I had a wonderful time last night. Thank you."

This seems to knock him out of his indecisive stupor, and he reacts immediately. His arms come around me, and Benjamin gives me a kiss that is anything but a goodbye. It feels very much like an invitation to stay, and that delights me more than I care to admit.

But I can't since I really do need to get going. When I pull away and he releases me, his expression is reluctant. I know mine matches.

"Tonight?" he asks simply. "Wicked Horse? Or would you like to come back here?"

Tilting my head, I give him another apologetic smile, this one more regretful than the last. "Actually, I would love to do either with you, but I can't. I actually have plans I can't back out of."

It's vague, I know—the explanation of my prior commitment. But we are not in the type of relationship that requires me to explain myself. Not that I have anything to hide, but well... I don't want to move too far out of the box we'd put around ourselves. It's risky to say the least.

"Oh," Benjamin says, and I can tell he's slightly put off. Not in a mad or angry way, but I can tell it never occurred I might not want to spend every night with him. He gives me an understanding smile, though. "Sure, I understand. Another night when it's convenient."

I find myself not wanting him to have any doubts about my desires, and I don't want him feeling rejected. Risk be damned, I decide to explain.

"Please know if I could get out of these plans, I would. I would much rather spend the evening with you. But Walsh is up for some businessman-of-the-year award, and Jorie asked me to attend it several weeks ago.

I promised her, and I can't back out. Why I agreed is beyond me because I hate these things. I won't know anyone there. Even though Jorie wants me there, she'll have to stick by Walsh's side most of the evening. So I'm sure you can understand this is not going to be pleasant for me."

I'm completely blown away by Benjamin's next words. "Would you like me to go with you? I'm assuming you can bring a plus one."

I blink at him stupidly. An array of emotions flutters through me. Thrilled he would offer. Worried at the same time. I would love to be able to do normal things with Benjamin, but I can't help but wonder if he's moving us toward failure. Can he really be ready for more?

Am I?

"I mean," he continues as if he needs to reassure me. "You did me a solid when you went with me to that charity gala. The least I can do is return the favor to you."

"I wouldn't want to impose," I rush to say, offering him a way to back out gracefully.

But fuck, I really would like him to come with me.

"You're not," he replies quickly. "It would be my pleasure."

This is it—an intense change of circumstances between us.

Tilting my head, I say, "I thought you wanted

boundaries. I thought we had agreed this was only about sex. You going on a date with me to an event is distinctly not within those boundaries."

Benjamin gives me a rakish grin. "If it helps, I do plan on fucking you after. Hell, maybe even at the event in one of the bathrooms or in the parking lot."

I can't help the laugh that pops out of me. I haven't seen this lighthearted, funny side of Benjamin before.

I like it way too much.

Benjamin takes my hands, giving them a squeeze. "Listen, maybe we should just play things by ear. I'm not going to lie. It seemed natural for me to offer to go with you tonight. It surprised even me. What I do know is I want to see you. I like being around you. So why not?"

"It's sort of like we're friends with benefits," I point out with a grin.

"Maybe. I haven't been a friend to so many people in a long time. Not sure I'm any good at it."

"Well, I can tell you that you're very good at the benefits part," I say with a laugh. "I'm willing to try the friend thing to see how that goes."

Benjamin's hand comes to the back of my neck, and he pulls me toward him for a kiss.

Just before our lips meet, he murmurs, "Friends with benefits. I'm liking the sound of that."

CHAPTER 23

Benjamin

F ANCY DINNERS, AWARD shows, charity events, operas… I've done it all throughout my life. It was nothing to put on a tux or suit to go out for a high-class evening.

It's a bit different for Elena. She comes from a working-class background, a single woman who owns her own business and lives a modest life. She has the misfortune of having a best friend who married into riches and a new lifestyle, and, to her consternation, wanted her to be part of that life, too.

I'd wanted to drive to Henderson to pick Elena up, but she felt that was silly given we planned to stay at my new apartment the evening after the event. So she drove here to me. It offended my notions of gentlemanly manners, but I don't know why. We're just friends with benefits. Nothing wrong with Elena driving here to meet me so I can escort her to an event, right?

I choose to meet her in the parking lot of my apartment rather than letting her come in. If she comes in, chances are I won't let her out and we'll miss the event.

She doesn't disappoint as she steps out of her little car that has almost a hundred thousand miles on it. Her ivory cocktail dress is strapless and incredibly elegant as it hangs in soft folds almost to her ankles. Her only jewelry is a pair of pearl earrings, and I'm wishing I had a strand of pearls to put around her neck. It would complement the dress and her skin tone, and my need to step up and accept this as something more than just friends with benefits.

I move toward her, my cane clicking on the concrete walkway. For the first time since I met Elena, I'm a little self-conscious of it. Before, I didn't give a fuck what anyone thought because I wasn't trying to impress a goddamn person.

But now, I wonder if Elena thinks it makes me less of a man. She's never said a word. Never even looks at it when we're walking together. She doesn't shy away from the scars on my leg, even spends time lovingly stroking them when she's sucking my cock.

She speaks first as we come face to face. "Don't you look handsome."

"Had to make an effort just so I could legit stand next to you and hold my head up high," I reply smoothly, taking in her dress a second time. "You're stunning."

I'm pleased when Elena blushes from my compliment, and it seems to chase my insecurities away. I hold my arm out, and she moves beside me to take it. She even thrusts her hip to the side, tapping it against mine playfully. "We do make a good-looking couple, that's for sure."

Yes, we do.

I lead Elena to my Audi, help her into the passenger seat, and I can feel the heavy press of her stare through the windshield as I walk around the front toward the driver's side.

When I get in, she turns in her seat to face me, putting her hand on my thigh. "Thank you again for going with me."

I smile back as I start the engine. "The evening has just started, but I'm confident in saying it's my pleasure."

♦

"WHY IS IT the Vegas elite give me the heebie-jeebies?" Elena asks out of the side of her mouth as we stand next to each other, sipping at our drinks. Wine for her and a bourbon for me, although my limit is two tonight since I drove. Ordinarily, I wouldn't care about drinking past that limit and just take an Uber home, but for some reason, that just doesn't appeal to me.

I've got it in my mind that driving Elena to my new home in my car at the end of what I'm just going to go ahead and admit is a date is going to be fulfilling for some reason. I can't overanalyze, and I decide to just go with it.

"As a former member of the heebie-jeebies club," I say dryly as my gaze scans the room, "I think it's because they're so unapproachable. So into themselves."

Elena's laugh is light and tinkling. "I'm glad you renounced your membership."

It's true I'm no longer a member of the inner circle. I let my country club membership expire, I don't golf with the "guys" anymore, and my social game got flushed because I had no interest in it. Throwing dinner parties was sort of April's thing, so I don't miss that in the slightest.

Maybe the golf. I truly did love that.

"I imagine it was difficult watching Jorie enter into this world," I say.

She tilts her chin, eyes meeting mine, and shrugs. "She's still the same old Jorie. And Walsh is cool, but when you're a member of this level of society, you do have to play along with these folks. I get it. Walsh does business with most of them, and a lot of back scratching goes on."

That's true. Most of these social events are just cover for the genuine business that happens among the Vegas elite.

"So what's your idea of a good social get-together?" I ask Elena, because the only thing I know about her so far is she's best friends with Jorie. I don't know much about her friends otherwise.

"A backyard barbeque," she answers without hesitation, a grin on her face that looks like she's even at this moment, perhaps fondly, remembering just such an event. Her voice is a little dreamy. "Ribs, burgers, dogs on the grill. Cold beer. Music blaring. Kids running through the backyard sprinkler to stay cool on a hot day."

I can see it. Elena wearing cut-off shorts and maybe a bikini top, because I'll always picture her being sexy. Talking and laughing with family and friends. Running through the sprinkler with the kids because why wouldn't she? She's fun, spirited, and isn't afraid to be silly.

April would have never done that, and I have immediate guilt for comparing them. My mind doesn't often go there, and that's mostly because I've always had April firmly locked up and tucked away.

But it's true. April would have been dressed in a pretty summer dress, hair and makeup done perfectly, and she would have been content to watch the kids getting wet and laugh. But she would have never joined in.

"What about you?" she asks, and it breaks me out of my thoughts. I blink, taking a small sip of my bourbon so I can relish the taste and not the effect.

Another memory hits, and I can't help but smile. "My parents used to have backyard barbecues all the time while I was growing up. But it was always chicken wings. My dad loved them, and my mom was exceptionally good at making them. They were never big affairs—just a few close friends—but I can still smell those wings smoking on the grill."

"Did kids run through the sprinklers?" she asks, eyes sparkling.

"We had a pool," I say with a laugh. "We were all swimming."

"Such an elitist," she drawls playfully. "But sounds like fun times."

"They were." I remember them fondly, and I realize... I haven't been allowing myself to focus on any of my memories, including childhood. I've shut everything from the past off, not just those surrounding April and Cassidy.

A sudden longing for my mother hits me. It's so intense my injured leg starts to shake a bit in weakness. I grip the handle of my cane, leaning a little heavier on it.

My mother and I were super close prior to the accident. I was the quintessential mama's boy. So was my older brother for that matter. We both love our dad, but it was our mother we always turned to in hard times.

She was the one who never left my side in the hospital.

She was the one who told me about April and Cassidy.

She handled dealing with my doctors, paying my personal bills for me, and then handling funeral arrangements. She did all of that while I systematically shut down my emotions, which also meant cutting her out as well.

She took care of me while I offered her nothing in return, and the regret is intensely painful.

After I recovered enough to handle things on my own, she returned to Michigan at my insistence. She respected my space, even though she hadn't liked the way I had pushed her away.

But she's never given up on me. She's always called and texted, and if I didn't answer or respond, she let me be and just tried again the next day. Her persistence never annoyed me as I understood it was beyond her control. It wasn't fair when I asked her to stop acting like my mother. And if she was annoyed or hurt by my refusal to act like a loving son, she never let me know it.

I should call her. Just out of the blue, for no other reason than just to hear her voice. I can't remember the last time I did that, and it's because I've been a selfish fuck this past year, only worrying about myself.

I make a mental note that my mom will be next on my priority list tomorrow morning after Elena leaves. It will be a step I can take to start repairing that relationship as well.

"Elena," an excited female voice cuts through my thoughts. I turn to see Jorie and Walsh approaching.

The women hug hard, rocking slightly back and forth. It's clear by the expressions on their faces they're incredibly tight. This past week, Elena had shared a little bit more about their friendship, dating back to child-hood. Elena took Jorie in when her first marriage collapsed, and she's also the one who introduced her to The Wicked Horse.

Looking at Walsh and Jorie now, it's hard to believe they're members there. Or were members. Elena had told me they don't go anymore.

Which I can sort of understand. I originally went to The Wicked Horse to fulfill a specific purpose.

To have feeling.

I have that now with Elena. I don't need the sex club trappings to experience it, although I have to say it's still a hell of a lot of fun to go there with her.

"Benjamin," Walsh says with a wide smile of greet-ing, sticking his hand out. I expertly take the weight onto my bum left leg, flipping my cane to hold it under my arm, and transfer my drink into my left hand. My right hand grips onto his for a hearty shake.

"Good to see you," I reply smoothly, then lift my drink slightly. "Congrats on the award."

Walsh snorts. "You know I don't give a shit about that stuff, man."

I can't help but laugh, because yeah... even though Walsh plays the game, I know hanging with the Vegas elite on an enjoyable level really isn't his thing. It's only business.

Jorie and Elena start chatting, even sidestepping a few feet away from us. I don't like the distance between us, and I'm wondering why. Because I'm now forced to talk to Walsh or because I just like having her near me?

Regardless, Walsh doesn't give me an opportunity to analyze it further. "You up for some golf next weekend?"

I blink in surprise. I haven't golfed since the accident or even considered it. The excuse comes quickly to my lips. "I'm so out of practice. I'd just hold you back."

"Got to get back into the swing of things sooner or later," he replies, his gaze holding steady to me before dropping briefly to my leg. "Unless that thing's holding you back?"

Some would take offense, but I like he's not afraid to call it as he sees it. I look down at my leg, my cane still under my arm before giving him my regard again. "Probably not. I mean… I use it more for taking weight off to keep the pain away, so I don't have to take any medicine. Sort of just used to it now."

"So pop a few Tylenols and let's do it," he replies, his tone of voice suggesting he's not going to take "no" for an answer.

"Okay," I reply on a whim. I mean, why the fuck not? I like Walsh, and I'd love to get back to golfing. I'm probably going to be hurting like a motherfucker after, but so what. "But how about we start out with just nine holes?"

"Sounds like a plan," Walsh replies with a laugh, then his gaze slides over to Jorie and Elena for a moment. "I know you've been through a lot. Elena's a strong girl, but you need to be careful with her."

I jerk in surprise, moving the end of my cane back down onto the floor for support. It's just more of a natural feeling to me.

My eyes study Walsh's face, who is still regarding the women. A pleasant smile to go along with the words that are clear in their intent.

"You don't have to worry about me breaking her heart if that's what you're worried about." I take a sip of my bourbon. "Elena and I are both the same. We don't want a deep involvement. We've actually had quite a bit of discussion about it."

Walsh turns his attention back to me, a sly smile on his face. "And that's exactly why you have to be careful. The mere fact you need to have discussions about it tells me it could become a problem. And I know how great Elena is. It could become a big problem for you."

"That's not something you need to tell me," I mutter as I take in her beauty while she talks to Jorie. I never can seem to get enough of looking at her. "I figured that out all on my own."

"Just don't lie to yourself, Benjamin," Walsh says, then starts to move toward Jorie. He gives me one last lingering glance, so his words sink in. Then he smiles. "See you on the links—Saturday, okay?"

After I nod, Walsh whisks Jorie away to make social rounds.

Elena moves back to my side, giving me a sympathetic smile. "That didn't look too painful."

"Really?" I reply with an undercurrent of sarcasm. "Because he was all up in my business."

"Poor baby," she coos, and I snicker.

"Actually, he wants to play golf so I'm going to give a try," I say blandly.

"Oh, that's awesome," she replies with a full-on blinding smile.

"He also thinks you and I are fooling ourselves," I say.

The smile slides away, and she tilts her head in confusion.

"That you and I are just about the sex," I explain. "That's all we've got."

Elena waves her hand in dismissal. "Well, that's simply not true. We decided we're friends with benefits."

"We're more, and you know it," I reply, shocked by my own whim of an admission.

Elena's eyes go wide. "Are we?"

I give a sigh, unsure of myself again. "I don't know. I just know it's more than sex, and it's more than just a friendship. But what that means, I have no clue. Do you have any brilliant thoughts?"

Grinning, Elena shakes her head. "That sounds about right, but I don't know what it means either."

"Great," I mutter dramatically, taking another small sip of my liquor, once again just enjoying the taste. "The blind leading the blind."

"We're hot messes." She laughs, slipping her arm through my elbow and leaning into me slightly.

I don't even compensate by pressing harder onto my cane. Instead, I take her weight all on my own and hold it without a thought as to my ability to do so.

CHAPTER 24

Elena

HARD TO BELIEVE how radically things have changed in a week. It's once again an early Sunday morning. As I come awake, I stretch. Hands above my head, I lengthen my body and feel my fingers brush against my wrought-iron headboard.

A smile plays at my lips as I remember how diligently Benjamin worked last night to tie me to the metal scrolls. Arms corner to corner, legs spread wide and secured with silk rope. He fucked me so hard that I thought my bed would break. Luckily, it remained secure.

As I stretch, my legs brush against Benjamin, who is currently sleeping on his stomach. Neither of us are long-term night cuddlers and have our comfortable sleeping positions, but we somehow always end up with our legs entwined.

It's been a week since we went from a "sex only" relationship to a dating one, and I have to say, I'm incredibly happy. Benjamin has made it easy on me to go out on a limb with him because we've both been transparent with our reasons for being reluctant in the first place.

I realize it's a bit of a bigger leap for Benjamin than me. My fears in getting involved with someone stem from repeatedly being taken advantage of. Sure, there was hurt involved, but I was tired of being disgusted in myself for falling for yet another codependent leech.

Benjamin has suffered such intense and emotional loss, and his fears are a whole hell of a lot scarier than mine. And when I saw him willing to take that risk, to admit he's ready to finally open himself up to possibility, there was just no way I couldn't not leap off that ledge with him.

We've settled into a routine based on our work schedules. If Benjamin has surgery, we stay at his place the night before. If he has regular patient rounds or office appointments, we stay at my place. Benjamin never once tried to make it seem like his job is more important. If anything, he's recognized I work as hard in my career path as he does. Never once has he made me feel less than him by virtue of what we do for a living.

When I slide my foot along the inside of Benjamin's calf, he stirs. He's not a heavy sleeper, and he always wakes up if I do. I'll roll out of bed at two to go pee, thinking I'm being stealthy, and he'll sit straight up to ask, "What's wrong? Are you okay?"

It's sweet, but I also bet it's because Benjamin is a

worrier by nature. I suspect sleep brings him terrible
things sometimes. I've been woken up a few times this
past week to him having what I believe to be nightmares.
Restless tossing, shaking, and muttering. He would then
jerk awake, seemingly gasping for breath. I'd lay still,
pretending to be asleep so as not to embarrass him that
I'd witnessed such a thing.

Benjamin would fall back asleep, usually after moving just a little closer to my body, sliding his leg in
between mine so we were touching.

I move my foot back down Benjamin's leg, playfully
rubbing my toe against his arch. His leg jerks from the
tickling sensation, and he mutters, "Go back to sleep,
Elena. You wore me out last night."

I snort. It was totally the other way around. I tickle
his foot again.

Benjamin moves lightning fast, flipping to his side
facing me. His hands go to my ribs, and he starts to
tickle me mercilessly.

I laugh, screech, claw at his hands, kick with my legs,
and try to squirm away. "Benjamin... stop it. I'm going
to pee."

His eyes are heavy with sleep, hair all in disarray. His
beard is thicker in the mornings, making him look older
and wiser, but it's the devilish sparkle in his eye I cherish
because I love this playful side of his.

His hands still, and he pulls me in close. Lips to my
neck, he runs a prickly kiss along my skin. One of his

hands takes mine, then leads it between us. My knuckles brush against something hard and velvety.

"Look what I woke up with," Benjamin murmurs against my neck.

He takes my hand, guides my fingers around his length, then makes me squeeze. I sigh, and he groans.

Lifting his head, Benjamin pins me with his soulful eyes that are filled with yearning for me. "Don't go to church this morning. Let's stay in bed all day pleasuring each other."

My toes curl over the sinfulness within his tone. More than ever, I should go to church because of how much that turns me on.

"Stay with me, Elena," he says as he gently rubs his bearded cheek against mine. "Let me have you all day. We can watch old movies and eat junk food in bed."

The naked want in his voice gets to me, and it's not just about sex. He wants to spend time with me.

"Okay," I say without any thought. "Let me just text my mom to let her know."

Benjamin immediately lets go of my hand so I can release his cock, and I roll away from him to nab my phone off the nightstand. Pressing an elbow into the mattress, I put my thumbs to the screen and shoot out a quick text to my mom. *Not feeling well this morning. Passing on church. Will call you later.*

I hit send without a moment's regret. While I love going to church—the same one I've attended with my family all my life—I don't feel bad when I miss a service. My relationship with God is personal, and it extends far beyond the walls of the chapel.

I don't even feel a twinge of guilt I'm forsaking church in favor of spending a day in bed with a man I'm not married to. My God is forgiving and wants me to be happy, and that's not merely an excuse. I honestly believe it. I'll gladly accept my penance after confession, because I think Benjamin needs this as much as I do.

I set my phone back on the nightstand, first turning my ringer off because today has now become Benjamin's and I don't want to be disturbed by anyone. I roll back toward him, only to be met with his mouth. His arms go around me, and his kiss is deep and claiming.

He's back in my hand again, hard yet silky soft, and I start stroking him leisurely. I'm not in a rush to get him off, and the slow glide of Benjamin's hand over my lower back tells me he's not in a rush either.

Lazy kisses, teasing touches, soft sighs. We extend our foreplay far beyond where it's ever gone before. I stroke his cock to the point where he starts thrusting in my hand before I retreat, then move my hands to his chest. Benjamin fondles between my legs, teasing with whispered touches that have my hips gyrating, then he stops to concentrate only on our kiss.

It seems like hours later, but there comes a time where our breaths are ragged and we're vibrating with need. When we're on our sides facing each other,

Benjamin pulls me in close. His hand goes to my thigh, and he jacks my leg up past his hip. I reach down, take him in my hand, and guide him to my entrance. We both suck in a breath and hold it as his head breaches my wet pussy and his eyes lock onto mine just before he jams in deep.

"Damn, that feels good," I moan as my head falls back and my eyes flutter close.

"Perfect," he groans, then starts to thrust against me.

I just hold on, arms locked around his neck and my breasts pressed flat against his chest. Benjamin holds my leg up high, fingers digging down into me. I feel every inch of his cock claiming me, and I know how easily I can get lost in this man.

Benjamin fucks me thoroughly. He's come to know my body well. Knows just how deep I can take it and the exact type of touch on my clit to make me explode.

I cling to him as I come, crying out my release, and Benjamin tips right over after me. I love the way he plants deep, spills into me, and shudders in complete ecstasy while murmuring my name.

Oh my... that was so good. My ears are still slightly ringing. Benjamin rolls to his back, taking my weight with him. He locks his arms around me, and he presses his face into my neck while his breathing regulates.

My eyes are heavy, and I love the idea of a lazy day. Falling back asleep only to wake up again to make love. Maybe I'll take him in my mouth and wake him up next time, or better yet—

"Hola… Elena," my mother calls out from somewhere near my front door. My bedroom door is closed, but her voice rings through loud and clear because she's not a soft-spoken woman.

"Holy shit," I rasp in shock as I roll off Benjamin, protectively bringing the sheet over my breast.

To my horror, my bedroom door opens and there stands my mom.

Five-foot-four inches of Hispanic sass and fire, Irma Costieri stares in wide-eyed shock. Her gaze slides over to Benjamin. I have no clue what he's doing as I'm terrified to look at him. All I can do is stare at my mother as my entire body flushes with embarrassment.

Her gaze returns to me, her chin lifting. "I came over to check on you. You never miss church because you're not feeling well, and I was worried."

"Oh, geez," I groan as I slap my hands over my face. I split my fingers a tiny bit to peek out at my mom. "I'm so sorry I lied. I didn't think you'd come here."

Now, my mother knows I'm not a virgin because we had the "sex" talk when I was in high school, which opened transparency between us as I got older. She's seen me have serious relationships—even two where my boyfriends had moved in with me. But I've never had my mom walk in on me while with a man, especially not after I'd lied about why I wasn't going to church.

"You should have just said you were busy," my mom

replies drolly, then smiles at Benjamin. "Hello."

"Hello," Benjamin says, and I want to smack him. I can hear the humor in his voice. When I risk a glance at him... I can tell by the expression on his face he's not embarrassed in the slightest.

There's an awkward silence that follows before my mom finally turns her attention to me. "Aren't you going to formally introduce us? Or is it too much for a girl to want her mother to meet the man who is occupying her bed?"

"Mamá," I exclaim.

She merely crosses her arms, giving me a stubborn look.

Relenting, I wave to the man beside me. "This is Benjamin. Benjamin... that's my mother, Irma Costieri."

Benjamin pushes himself up in bed, keeping a hold of the sheet at his waist. He sticks a hand out. "Pleasure to meet you, Mrs. Costieri."

My mom isn't charmed by him in the slightest. Her upper lip curls a bit in a sneer, and she refuses to shake his hand. She does at least give him a slight nod before turning back to me.

"So this is more important than church? Some man you had over last night? Someone who doesn't mean anything to you—"

I cut her off. "We've been seeing each other for over a month, Mamá. He's not just some man."

She sniffs in disbelief because this is not something I would do... hide a potential love interest. But my mom doesn't know how disenchanted I've become with love. How I've only been engaging in meaningless sex before Benjamin.

She's not buying it, and her disapproval rolls off her in waves. The daughter she knew, raised, and loved is not about to accept I'd keep a man secret from her for a month.

While I can't tell her how we met or even the why of it, because she'd never understand, I can distract her from her current ire.

"Benjamin's a neurosurgeon, Mamá."

And there it is... her inner mother who has only ever wanted the absolute best for her daughter comes out. A smile splits her face, and she studies Benjamin with newfound appreciation.

Her hand shoots out and she takes his, giving him a hearty welcome-to-the-family shake. "Benjamin... so very nice to meet you."

She then mouths ever so obviously, "A neurosurgeon?"

"Yes, Mamá," I reply with a smile, thinking she'll now forgive me for skipping church because I bagged someone good.

To my horror, though, she sits on Benjamin's side of the bed, right near his hip, and pats his leg. "Now, Benjamin... tell me all about yourself. Where are you from? How did you meet my Elena? And wow... a neurosurgeon. That's just so impressive."

"Mother," I practically screech as I sit up straight, holding the sheet to me for dear life. I point to the door. "Now is not the time for conversation. As you can see, we're um... well, we need... what I mean to say is..."

"Now isn't the best time," Benjamin intones, cutting over my prattle. "Maybe we can get dressed, then I can take you ladies out to breakfast or something."

God love that man, but I really could kiss him right about now as realization sweeps over my mom's face that she has overstepped her bounds.

She blushes clear up to the roots of her hair, then jumps off the bed as she stammers an apology. "Oh, where in the world are my manners?"

Benjamin chuckles, and I give him an elbow to the ribs.

My mom bobs her head. "You want to spend some time with your new man. I'll just get out of here and head to church."

"Okay, Mamá," I murmur, blowing her a kiss.

She turns sharp eyes to Benjamin. Points at him. "Next time... you come to church with Elena, okay? And after, you come to my house for tamales."

Benjamin inclines his head and gives her a warm smile, which my mom takes as an acceptance of her invitation. But I know that's not the case. Benjamin might be up for Mom's tamales—although it does seem to be a little soon to be introducing him to family—but no way in hell he'd go to church with us.

In fact, I could imagine Benjamin saying something like, "I wouldn't go see God if he was standing in your front yard."

That's all right. It's enough for me to know God loves him anyway.

If I'm not careful, I might end up feeling the same way.

CHAPTER 25

Benjamin

I T'S A PERFECT Fourth of July, and it's all because of Elena.

Yes, the sun is shining brightly, though sometimes blotted out by fluffy pristine clouds against a crystal blue sky.

Yes, I've found the perfect little cove on Lake Mead to toss anchor where we can take a break from skiing and the other revelers on the lake to have some privacy with each other.

Yes, every day I spend with her, I become more enchanted. I don't regret my decision to let things progress with her.

And yes... my life seems to be taking an upswing because of this woman.

I try to just enjoy the sun. Let myself get lost in the music. I've got my earbuds on, my favorite classic rock playlist blaring, and I'm reclined on one of the padded benches just chilling.

Elena is on the bow of the boat, stretched out on a towel and working on a glorious tan. While the cove we're in is private enough, it's not completely secure. Otherwise, I'd encourage her to go full nude. As it is, the little string bikini she's wearing makes me happy to stare at the absolute perfection of her body while knowing it's all mine to do with whatever I want, whenever I want.

That's because Elena likes whatever I do to her, whenever I do it.

The perfect relationship has only been getting better.

I figure if there were ever a time when things could have dampened it was when her mom burst in on us moments after we'd just finished some amazing fucking. My heart was still galloping when Irma Costieri opened that bedroom door, and things could have gone south fast.

Not because of the embarrassingly awkward situation, but mainly because it's a big to deal to meet the parents of the person you're dating. It wasn't something I know Elena had ever even considered doing, and I wasn't in a place to even think about it with my mom.

Hell, she and I are just now back on good terms. We're communicating regularly. I'd made the first step and reached out to her like I'd promised myself a week ago.

It was emotional as fuck, and I wasn't prepared to confront those feelings. I knew I had to apologize for my behavior. That was my big goal, and I pulled it off without a hitch. I thought after that, I could keep the convo light but make it clear I wanted to get back to normal. Instead, I wanted to cry like a damn baby when my mother wouldn't let me apologize. She wouldn't give me her forgiveness because she had declared none was needed.

She had merely said, "Benjamin... I love you. You have nothing to be sorry for. You merely survived as best you could. As your mother, I fully support the way in which you had to do it. It was your way, and that's all that matters to me."

Fuck, she slayed me. Showed me what being a parent truly means.

Exemplified the theory of unconditional love with just a few words.

Since then, things have been easy. Daily communications, usually via text, but that has more to do with me being so damn busy. One by one, I made other connections. My dad reached out. Then my brother. We're all back talking again.

It's breezy conversation as if they know I can't handle much more than that, but one day—hopefully soon—I'll have the balls to tell them how sorry I am for shutting them out.

I'll try to explain why I'd done what I had. Hopefully, they'll be as understanding as my mother.

Elena shifts, arching her back slightly, which thrusts her breasts up. They're fantastic, by the way. Truly my favorite part of her body. I could spend hours worshiping them.

When her head swivels, I can tell she's staring at me through her dark sunglasses. Her lips curve up at the corners, and she asks me something.

I can't hear her because of the music blaring in my ears so I pull my buds out. She repeats what she just said. "Why are you staring?"

"Because you're the best thing to look at out here?" I reply truthfully. "By a long shot."

Elena pushes up to her elbows, scanning the scenery. It really is a beautiful day, and the water has been like glass. I was pleased to find out Elena likes to ski. I used to spend a lot of time on this boat with April, but not so much after we had Cassidy. She was a little too young for water sports, but we would come out on occasion and just tool around a bit.

It feels good to be out again.

Feels good to be experiencing life.

"Why did you go to the Wicked Horse?" I ask, and she raises her eyebrow. "You've never told me why. Only you weren't interested in a relationship."

I can't see her eyes behind those sunglasses, but I get the impression she's blinking in surprise.

Her hesitancy in answering leads me to believe she might have suffered a terrible loss the way I did, and now I regret asking something she might not be ready to talk about.

But Elena merely gives a dismissive shrug as if it's not all that interesting of a story. "I had been dating a string of extreme losers."

Well, that explains exactly nothing. "How so?

"Just got tired of trying to find someone genuine. I used to get taken advantage of quite a bit."

My protective instincts kick in, and I suppress a growl. I now want the names and addresses of anyone who would dare think they could hurt Elena. She doesn't notice, though, only leans back on her towel as she continues. "It was always the same. They'd start off cherishing me. Romancing me. Sweeping me off my feet. The next thing I know, I'm doing everything. Caring for them, paying for shit, and being their psychotherapist so they can deal with mommy issues or something."

"Emotional leeches," I surmise.

"Pretty much," she replies softly. "I got tired of needing to always fix them. I had to be responsible for their personal happiness. Which is fine if it's a two-way street, but it was always all take and no give. Codependency at its finest. It drained the life out of me every time. But to answer your original question, I got tired of feeling like shit about it. Hating them and hating myself for letting it happen. So I heard about The Wicked Horse. As you know, I really like sex. So I thought it would be a suitable alternative to my current life choices."

"Got it," I murmur, letting my gaze wander out over the sparkling water.

"I don't consider you broken, Benjamin," Elena says, and I snap my head up. She takes her sunglasses off, turning her body to go to one elbow so she can look directly at me. "You're the least broken person I know."

"How can you even say that?" I ask, astonished by such a bold proclamation.

"How can I not?" she replies, her brows furrowing in consternation. "You survived a horrible accident. Suffered incredible loss. And yet, you've managed to continue giving top-notch medical care in an incredibly specialized field. Sure, you may have been a withdrawn dick to many people over time, but you've broken free of that. Taken risks. Given me a chance. Offered me unlimited pleasure. Smiled. Stood up to my Latina mother while naked. Like I said... least broken man I know, Benjamin."

"Your mother coming in your room was incredibly weird," I say with a grin, trying to lighten the mood up a bit. I can't pretend her words of affirmation aren't packing a pleasurable punch to my gut.

She smiles, but her eyes are still locked on me with serious intent. "Seriously... you're handling your issues. You're a strong man. I can tell."

"Haven't felt that way in a long time," I admit. What I don't admit is she makes me feel strong.

"But I also feel compelled to make sure you under-stand," she continues, "that if you ever wanted to talk about things with me, I'm there for you. I really like you,

Benjamin, and I wasn't expecting this to be anything. Yet, it's turning into everything. You can be strong and still lean on someone. And I can still accept the weight of another's problems without having to give up everything of myself. I think that's something I just recently learned."

Fuck if she's not saying all the right things. Validating me without pressuring me. Comforting me without making me feel weak. Offering a new layer to our relationship that threatens to put me on the edge of jumping all the way in with her.

Am I ready for that?

Brandon seems to think so.

In addition to reconnecting with my family, Brandon and I have made strides the last two weeks. It started with an apology from me for canceling on a surgery and dropping off the face of the earth for a few days. I had to make sure he knew I was a reliable medical partner and put any doubts to rest.

He accepted the apology stiffly and without any real enthusiasm. And then, without any forethought or planning or even any real understanding until that moment that Brandon needed a different type of apology.

"I'm sorry for abandoning our friendship," I'd told him, and I could have knocked him over with a feather in that moment. It was obvious by the expression on his face. "I put up walls, pushed those closest to me away, and as my best friend, that meant you. And I'm sorry for the hurt I've caused, and I'm thankful you've not booted me out on my ass yet."

That started a discussion that eventually led down the path to Elena. As we spent precious moments reconnecting, he wanted to know about her. It was clear he credits her with my transformation.

And while we still had repairing to do, I didn't mind sharing her with him.

Metaphorically, of course.

I admitted it had started out just as sex, but it had absolutely progressed to something else. Something more. Something I couldn't quite define yet, but I knew was transformative.

This pleased Brandon a lot. He's a happily married man, and he wants me to be happy as well. He equates happiness to a secure relationship. While I've experienced that before, and I agree with it, that's still a little more than I was willing to consider at this point.

But there's a reason he's my best friend, and he proved it by narrowing in on something that must have been causing me some internal strife.

"April would want you to move on," he'd said to me with certainty. "You know that, right?"

I just stared at him, for the first time considering what April would think. How had I not done so before? Is it because I'd so lost my belief in God and Heaven I didn't even think April existed anymore?

But if she did… what would she want?

"She'd want you to have another shot at happiness," Brandon had said quietly. "A shot at love. Kids. Everything. In fact, she'd be disappointed if you stopped living your best life."

He was right.

He *is* right.

I know it with certainty. While we never discussed dying and what would happen after, I know April loved me and to love me would mean my happiness was paramount to her.

Just as I know had I predeceased her, I'd have wanted her to fall in love again. Make more babies. Grow old with someone devoted to her.

"I like you too," is all I can manage to say to Elena. Words can barely express what I do feel for her, but they're simple and truthful. They don't compare with what she's said to me and the way she's validated me.

But I'll try to get better at it.

All part of my journey to rediscover my life.

Smiling, she crooks her finger. "Why don't you come over here and rub some oil on my back?"

Her tone is husky, inviting, and I know she wants me to rub other places as well.

That is something I can totally get on board with.

CHAPTER 26

Elena

WHEN I GLANCE at my watch, I'm satisfied I'm running a bit ahead of schedule. I took the afternoon off from work to go to a doctor's appointment with my mom. She's been suffering with some knee pain that's gotten progressively worse, and they're attempting an injection on her today.

Normally, my father would go with her, but he's in Los Angeles on a business trip. None of my brothers can be counted on to step in, so I gladly volunteered.

I love my brothers, I really do. Five strong, smart, and capable men who don't have a freaking clue on how to help with our parents as they get older. Granted, my mom has always been a bit of an enabler, rushing in to do everything for her boys.

Maybe I inherited a bit of that from her. Maybe I tend to do too much for the men in my life, and that turns them codependent on me. Maybe that makes me a magnet for a certain type of man.

But no… Benjamin isn't like that at all. Despite the traumas he's suffered, he's yet to try to latch on to me as the fixer of his woes. I've learned he has a deep well of quiet strength he has been pulling from to drag himself out of the darkness. He is truly the strongest person I know. It makes him even more attractive to me, despite some of the fears that still hold him back just a tiny bit.

Yes, things are now moving a bit faster, yet I'm not scared by it. Benjamin is just so different—not just from any man I've known, but from any person. He's the most self-aware person I've ever met. He knows his weaknesses and what draws out his worst, and, when asked, he's utterly transparent about those things. He is never afraid to admit his failures or flaws.

At any rate, I completed my mission to take Mom to the doctor. Helped her home, put her leg up, and made her a late lunch. Left the remote control and a cup of tea near her, then jetted back out. I have to pick up a new prescription the orthopedic prescribed, then I'm off for a quick shopping trip for a new dress because tonight, things are advancing just a bit more between Benjamin and me.

We've been invited to dinner at Brandon and Colleen's house. This is significantly important for a few reasons. First and foremost, Benjamin has repaired his relationship with his best friend. Maybe not fully, but for the most part. I know this because he not only told me about the conversation where he apologized, but also because each night we're together, over dinner or a drink or while watching TV, he'll tell me a funny or interesting story about Brandon that had happened.

Point is… they are back in solid friendship territory; the past year is now just a memory for them that hopefully won't be something to linger on.

Tonight is also important because Benjamin and I are stepping into his former social circle as a "couple". The invitation was for Benjamin and me to come to Brandon and Colleen's house for a backyard barbeque. It's just going to be the four of us. Their kids are off to spend the weekend with Colleen's parents. The barbecue is going to be casual, but I want a pretty summer dress to wear.

I want to look pretty for Benjamin so he's proud to have me as his date. After I get my new dress, I'll have enough time to run home, get showered and put together, then drive into Vegas to meet Benjamin at his apartment. He offered to come get me, but we're staying at his place tonight so Jorie and I can go baby shopping tomorrow in Vegas and it's silly for him to come all this way just to get me.

I pull up to the pharmacy, which is a small, independently owned business. It's in this cool outdoor shopping center that has eclectic stores like one that sells nothing but flavored olive oils and spices, or another that does high-priced juiced drinks. My parents and I always try to patron locally owned businesses, as my dad is a small business owner himself. He owns a home security system franchise.

MyRx is one of the corner shops, and it's owned by a young woman named Nicki Palino. She runs the place all by herself without a single employee to help. Of course, her hours are limited and she doesn't open until ten thirty, but she more than makes up for it by the extra customer service she provides. A trip in to see Nicki usually ends up a half-hour affair as she's just so fun to talk to.

When I open the glass door, a small chime goes off. I find it funny she has a doorbell as her shop isn't more than thirty-feet-by-thirty-feet in total. A long counter sits immediately to the right of the door, and the perimeter space behind it is lined with shelves holding the prescription medications she fills.

To the left is a small table with three chairs customers can sit in while they wait, along with a long-shelfed wall that holds over the counter medications.

Nicki's standing at a worktable behind the counter counting out tablets, and she raises her head with a smile on her face.

"Hey, Elena," she chirps in greeting. "I already got your mom's prescription filled."

That's the main reason I love coming here. I never have to wait. She's always so on top of things.

"Let me just finish this count," she says, returning to her task while I poke around a small lazy Susan display on the counter that holds a variety of essential oils.

I hear the door open, the chiming bell go off, and I turn to look over my shoulder at the next customer coming in.

Instead, I find the barrel of a gun pointed right at my face. Just beyond that, a masked man stands there.

"Back the fuck up," he orders, and I scramble to do as he says. He waves the gun toward the pass-through counter. "Get back there with her."

The man corrals me behind the counter with Nicki, and I start to walk straight toward her. Her eyes are wide with fear, and her skin has gone about five shades paler than her normal.

"Uh-uh," the man mutters, then grabs the collar of my shirt to yank me into him. "You stay near me."

"Just give him the money," I instruct Nicki in a calm voice. "It'll be okay."

The man lets out a hysterically high-pitched laugh, and Nicki just shakes her head as she murmurs. "He doesn't want money."

I go numb with true fear now, because if he doesn't want money, he must want Nicki and me. I consider striking out because I've always been taught to fight.

Instead, I'm dragged closer to Nicki by the gunman as he waves his gun at the shelves lined with medications. "You know the deal... all your oxy and percs. Adderall. Vicodin. And don't fucking leave anything behind."

What the fuck? He wants drugs?

And then it hits me... the street value has got to be way more valuable than just the cash from her register.

Nicki slowly reaches for a plastic bag, and the man screams. "Hurry, you dumb fucking bitch. I ain't got all day."

The man's arm goes around my neck to hold me closer, and I can feel his entire body vibrating. I wonder if he's just hyped up on adrenaline or if he needs some of those drugs himself.

Nicki moves faster, scrambling to one of the shelves. She starts tossing boxes into the bag.

"Faster," the man demands. Nicki falters, looking over her shoulder at us. The man moves the gun to my temple, and he presses the barrel there. "Fucking faster or I'll blow her goddamn head off."

Nicki pivots, then starts pulling inventory off the shelves faster. When the bag is half full, she turns to hand it to the man. He whips his head to the door, checks to see if anyone is near, and then swivels back to Nicki. Releasing his hold around my neck, he reaches out for the loot.

When it's in hand, he waves the gun, pointing at the floor. "All right... both of you on your knees with your faces away from me."

Nickie moves to the spot he indicates, then immediately starts to drop to her knees. I don't like the sound of putting myself into a position where he can shoot me execution style. Maybe I've watched too much of the *Sopranos* or something, but nope. Not going to happen.

I don't move a muscle.

"Get on your knees, bitch," he growls.

"No," I reply as I lift my chin, but my voice is shaking like a leaf. "You got your shit, now get out of here."

It comes so fast I have no time to react, dodge, or duck. His hand with the pistol cocks back and comes flying at me backhand style. Right across my temple. Stars explode in my eyes. The pain is blinding for a moment, but then I see my own blood spatter across Nicki's worktable as I go crashing to the floor.

My back is to him, and I wait for the bullet to come next.

Instead, the door chime goes off. My heart wrenches for whoever is getting ready to walk into this disaster. I hear the man curse, feet scuffling, and then someone else screams.

Nicki is at my side, gently turning me over so she can look at my head. "He's gone," she says. Someone else is now at my side, kneeling next to me. An older man with snowy-white hair in a buzz cut. He looks former military or police, and he has his phone pressed to his ear while he talks to 9-1-1.

"Yes, I just walked into a robbery at MyRx on Honey Camp Road. The assailant is gone, but there's an injured woman... looks like a head wound."

"He hit her with the gun," Nicki provides, then she pushes up and disappears. In moments, she's back with a towel to press to my bleeding head.

I try to sit up, but the man gently pushes me by the

shoulder to stay down as he continues to talk to the dispatcher.

"You've got a really bad laceration," Nicki advises me, her voice quavering. "I am so sorry, Elena."

I smile wanly. "Why? It's not like you planned this."

Her return smile is tremulous. "I just can't believe that happened. I mean... what the hell is wrong with people?"

"Indeed," I murmur, closing my eyes for a moment. My head hurts like a... well, like I'd just been pistol whipped.

Over the next twenty minutes, we're swarmed with police and crime scene investigators. Paramedics arrive and while I don't want to go in an ambulance, I'm sort of strong-armed into doing so by them and Nicki.

"You've got a nasty head wound, and you really should have a CT scan to make sure there's no bleeding on your brain," one told me.

That scared me a little, so I relented.

They load me onto a stretcher, and I feel foolish for it. I was sure I could walk, but they won't let me. They bandage up the wound, but they can't give me anything for the pain.

We can't leave until they get some of my basic information. Another paramedic works on starting an IV. While they're doing that, Nicki sits in the ambulance with me for support.

And then it occurs to me... I won't be shopping for a pretty dress or attending dinner at Brandon and

Colleen's tonight with Benjamin.

"Nicki… can you send a text for me?" I ask.

"Sure," she replies, then rummages through my purse for my phone.

I don't even consider calling Benjamin. He's busy at work seeing patients. Besides, I wouldn't even expect him to answer. This isn't an emergency, though, so I'm fine with a text.

I tell her exactly what to say on the text. After she sends it, she asks, "Do you want me to call your mom or someone else?"

"No," I say wanly. "Dad's out of town, and she just had a knee injection so she's not mobile right now. I'll call her later after the CT scan so I can assure her everything's fine."

"Want me to call anyone?" she presses.

I consider Jorie, but then decide against it. She'd worry, too, and I'm fairly sure there's nothing to worry about. Despite having a hell of a headache, I don't feel that bad. Nothing I would expect from such an injury— no dizziness or anything. I didn't even lose consciousness.

"I'll just wait until after they examine me, then I'll call one of my brothers," I say, although I'm not sure which one. They'll all panic to some extent.

Hell, maybe I'll just call an Uber to take me home. I am, after all, an independent woman.

Then why do I suddenly feel like crying and wish Benjamin was here at my side right now?

CHAPTER 27

Benjamin

"YOU'RE DOING REMARKABLY well, Sandy," I tell my patient as I give her a gentle pat on the knee. "I want you to come back in three months. If things stay the same, I'm going to release you."

"Thank you so much, Dr. Hewitt," she gushes, reaching down and squeezing my hand. "You saved my life."

"Well, you did all the hard work in recovery," I assure her, but it never feels old when a patient tells me that.

Reaffirms my purpose in life.

Grabbing my cane from the door where I normally leave it while examining a patient, I walk out of the exam room, move to the next door down the hall, and pull the patient chart from the plastic holder attached to the wall. As I flip through, orienting myself to the patient inside, my phone alerts me to an incoming text.

A text from an incredibly beautiful and sexy woman

who I can't seem to stop thinking about these days. I gave Elena her own text sound using one of the pre-programmed tones called "Ripple," which sounds like wind chimes.

Peaceful.

The way Elena often makes me feel, and I realize how much I've romanticized this woman if I program her text chime to induce the same feelings in me that she produces.

Shaking my head, I pull my phone out of my lab coat pocket. We don't ordinarily communicate during the day as we're both so busy, so it's unusual for her to text me. My curiosity has me wanting to look versus ignore.

My veins flood with what feels like ice when I read the text. *Please don't worry, but I was caught in the middle of an armed robbery at my pharmacy. I got hit in the head, and they're taking me to Henderson Hospital. I'm fine, but I wanted to let you know I won't be making dinner tonight. I'll call later to update you.*

"Are you fucking kidding me?" I growl into the empty hallway. She'll call to update me? She's fine?

She thought a fucking text was appropriate to reach out to me?

I slam the patient's file back into the folder. With long strides, I make my way to the reception desk. Three girls sit behind it. Before any of them can look up, I demand, "Where's Dr. Aimes?"

"Number four," one of the girls answers, but I'm already spinning away.

I make my way to the exam room, then take a deep breath before I knock. I'm bristling with rage, fear, and a weird, heavy weight on my chest.

Brandon opens the door, seeming surprised. Clearly the expression on my face concerns him as he immediately backs me into the hall, pulling the door shut behind himself. "What's wrong?"

"Elena was caught in the middle of some type of armed robbery. She's been injured, and I need to head to Henderson."

"Go," he says without hesitation. "I'll cover your patients."

That's all I need to hear. "Thanks, man. I owe you."

"I'll think of something good," he replies in an effort to make me smile. "Text me once you've been able to see her."

I throw my hand up in a wave of acknowledgment.

◆

I KNOW I'VE rattled the poor nurse who is leading me through the small emergency department. I'd come in demanding to see Elena, flashing my neurosurgery credentials like a fucking snob. It got me quick entrance, including the nurse leading me straight to the trauma doctor assigned to Elena's care.

He's just exiting a patient's curtained room, and the

nurse makes a hasty introduction. "Dr. Peele... this is Dr. Hewitt. He's Elena Costieri's boyfriend, and he just drove in from Vegas to see her."

"She's due back from CT any time now," Dr. Peele says as he sticks his hand out to me. He doesn't seem aggravated to see me.

"What's her status?" I ask gruffly. "I understand she had a head injury?"

He stares a moment before replying, "You know I technically can't give you any information as that's a breach of doctor/patient confidentiality. However, as a professional courtesy, she's stable and doing very well."

"Can you at least tell me what her GCS is?" I ask with annoyance. The Glasgow Coma Score is the first testing they would have done on her upon admission.

When he opens his mouth, I can tell by the expression on his face he's about to deny me, but then his eyes go to something over my shoulder. Turning, I see Elena being wheeled into a curtained room.

I don't hesitate, merely stride that way with my cane tapping on the tile floor, Dr. Peele on my heels. When I enter the curtained room, she's chatting with the attendant who had just transported her back from radiology. Her gaze slides over to me, widening with surprise.

"Benjamin," she murmurs as if she's seen a ghost. "What are you doing here?"

What am I doing here? Did she honestly just fucking

ask me that?

I ignore the question, taking just a moment to observe her physical injuries. I can't see much other than her temple is bandaged on the left side with blood seeping through. Her olive-toned skin is incredibly pale, but I imagine that's just exhaustion coming down off the adrenaline I know had to have been fueling her body.

"Tell Dr. Peele I have permission to discuss your case with him," I command, trying to ignore the hurt expression on her face.

No words of comfort. No hug. No sweet kiss. No concern for how she's feeling. Just an order to let me in so I can make sure she's okay.

Which is something she should have done from the start.

Elena nods at Dr. Peele. "You can talk to him about my medical situation."

I give my back to Elena, and Dr. Peele starts blabbing. GCS was excellent at a fifteen. That meant she had spontaneous eye-opening response, has been verbally responsive, and obeyed all commands for motor response testing.

"We're waiting on a plastic surgery consult for the laceration at her temple," Dr. Peele says as he moves to a standing computer station in the corner of the room. With a few taps on the keys, he's pulling up the CT scan results. "Looks like we're still waiting for radiology to read these—"

"I'm a neurosurgeon," I mutter as I push in beside him to study the digital pictures on the screen.

"Oh," Dr. Peele says, taking a step back to let me examine it more closely.

I take a few moments, critically studying the digital slices of Elena's brain. I always knew it would be a beautiful brain, and I'm relieved to see it intact with no evidence of swelling or bleeding.

"It looks good," I tell Dr. Peele, but of course, he'll need to verify it with the official review by the radiologist.

"I'm going to go check on the plastic surgery consult," he replies, leaving me alone with Elena.

Now I can stop being a doctor and be a concerned boyfriend, but for the life of me, I'm not sure what that means. I'm now battling a mix of relief she's fine with the terrorizing fear she could be dead right now.

I turn slowly, hating the look of distrust on her face. I've not behaved how she expected or needed.

When I take a step toward her, Elena's eyes well up with tears and my heart shreds. I move to the side of the bed, taking her hand in mind. I bend over, brush my lips over hers softly, and whisper, "You're okay. You're going to be fine."

And the whole time I do that, I have to restrain myself from fleeing. Because while part of me wants to comfort her, hold her, chase away all her scary memories, the truth is most of me wants to leave all this far behind.

The truth is it only took one bad thing happening to her to make me realize I could not survive losing her. Had he hit her a little bit harder, or had the gun gone off and she'd been shot, she could just as easily be lying in the morgue with me holding her hand.

I managed to pull myself back from that type of loss once, but I truly don't think I could survive it again.

These past few weeks, the way I put up walls and closed myself off to love, devotion, and relationships had seemed so silly, but now it doesn't seem stupid at all. Seems safe and secure to me.

I make myself stay, though, because I can't abandon her right now in her greatest need. I'm not that much of a selfish dick.

"You're going to be fine," I say again stupidly, knowing damn well she doesn't need my medical reassurances right now.

Elena nods, gives a tiny sniffle, and dashes the tears away with the back of her other hand. I reach behind me, grab a small chair, and pull it to the side of the bed so I can sit.

"How did it all happen?" I ask, dreading hearing the details.

Her voice is tremulous, unsure, and childlike. I've never seen Elena without her trademark confidence and sass. Right now, she's the victim of a violent crime and she's been reduced to it. I squeeze her hand a little tighter as she recounts what happened.

Christ... all for fucking drugs. She almost died so someone could get their fix.

"I thought he was going to execute us," she says softly, but the impact of those words feels like a nuclear explosion within me. My ears ring as she goes on to explain. "Told us to turn away from him. To get on our knees. I knew that meant he was going to shoot us, but he didn't have the fucking guts to look in our faces as he did it."

"Jesus fuck," I mutter.

"I wasn't going out without a fight. I refused, and that's when he hit me."

"Christ, Elena... I'm so sorry. You did the right thing."

Blinking back more tears, she nods. "Thank God someone walked in and spooked him. He just ran. God was looking out for me."

Those words don't sit well because I don't believe them. God doesn't do that. He doesn't save the innocent, at least not in my experience.

"Can you do me a favor?" Elena asks.

"Of course," I reply automatically, just as long as it's not to explain the myriad of fucked-up feelings I've got going on right now.

"Can you call my mom?" she asks, then nods over to her purse. "You'll have to grab my phone. I'm ashamed to say I don't even have her phone number memorized, and they don't have a landline anymore. I didn't want to worry her until I knew everything was going to be okay."

"Sure," I say as I stand from the chair. "But is she able to drive with her knee?"

"She'll get one of my brothers to bring her," she replies.

I get her phone, have Elena unlock it, and then pull up her mom's contact. Just as I'm about to dial, the plastic surgeon comes in. I step just outside the curtain while he examines Elena's laceration, keeping one eye on her as I call her mother.

It's not a pleasant conversation. Mrs. Costieri is hysterical at first, but I've dealt with many a patient's over-emotional family before. I'm able to talk her down quickly by assuring her that Elena is medically sound. We cut the call short so she can work on getting a ride to the hospital.

Back in the room, I introduce myself to the surgeon. She explains how she's going to stitch the laceration. It's in the delicate skin of her temple, running just to the front of her hairline. It's going to leave a visible scar, but hopefully one that's hard to see after she's done with it.

A nurse comes in with a tray, and I move to the other side of the bed while they work on Elena. She holds onto my hand tightly, particularly as they irrigate the wound. Once they apply the anesthetic, she relaxes, and I watch with a critical eye as the surgeon works to close the cut. Every delicate stitch she lays, I feel more despondent inside that this happened to the woman I've grown to care about so much.

It doesn't take long. Once we're alone again, I move the chair by her bed. I keep hold of her hand, sitting in silence with her. I don't even know what to say.

"Are you okay?" Elena asks.

I try to look confident when I meet her eyes, not guilty for having such confounding thoughts. "Of course. Why?"

"I don't know," she replies hesitantly. "You just look... like you'd rather be anywhere other than here. And that's okay if you need to go. I never expected you to leave work to come in the first place."

There it is.

My out.

And she handed it to me on a silver platter.

I don't even hesitate in fudging on the truth a bit. "I left in the middle of patient rounds. Brandon's covering, but—"

"Go," she says boldly, then pulls her hand from mine. "You shouldn't have done that. If you had called me, I could have assured you I was fine."

To my credit, I don't bound out of the chair. I sit there, unsure.

"Go take care of your patients," she says again, pointing toward the door. "My mom will be here soon, and I'll text you once I'm settled in at home later."

"Are you sure?" I ask, although I know she is. Elena doesn't offer things she doesn't mean.

"I'll be fine," she assures with a smile.

I push up from the chair, bend, and put my mouth against hers for a soft kiss. Closing my eyes, I memorialize the feel of her lips against mine, wondering if I'll ever feel this again.

CHAPTER 28

Elena

"**W**ANT ANYTHING ELSE?" my mom asks as she pops her head into the living room. I'm lying on her couch, flipping channels.

"I'm good, Mamá," I say without looking her way.

"Tea? Juice?"

I give her my attention and a reassuring smile. "I'm good. I promise."

Her return look is as worried as it was when she walked into the emergency room yesterday after Benjamin called her. But she's a mom. She'll never be reassured.

My mom insisted I come home with her rather than back to my house. Truth be told, I was really shaken up by the whole ordeal, so it didn't take much convincing. She kicked my youngest brother Luis out of his room so I could sleep there last night, and he took the couch. After all of us kids moved out, our parents downsized into a small three-bedroom ranch house. The master is for our parents, Luis was currently occupying the guest room, and the third is Dad's home office.

Luis didn't mind. Rather than take the couch, he went to stay with a friend. He'd just recently moved in with my parents after a bad breakup with a girlfriend he'd lived with. I expect he'll find a place of his own soon since he likes his space and privacy. I'm sure my parents will be happy as well, because while they love their six children dearly, they also like being empty nesters.

There's a light knock at the door before it opens. Few people would walk in without an invitation, but I know who it is, and she's always had an open-door policy here.

Tilting my head slowly over the arm of the couch, I smile when Jorie walks in carrying a huge vase of flowers. I'm not surprised when she hands them right to my mom saying, "Here you are, Mamá. To brighten your day."

This is typical Jorie. First, she calls my mom "Mamá" just like I do, but she *was* practically raised in this household. Jorie's mom died during childbirth and while her dad and older brother Micah did a good job of looking after her, she got "mom loving" over here.

Flowers delivered to the proper person, Jorie turns my way, her eyes raking over me critically. I know I don't look that bad other than the purple bruising at my temple and the line of delicate blue stitches along my temple. Still, she's evaluating my body language, facial expressions, and general vibe I'm giving off. My bestie knows me that well.

Sauntering my way, she mutters, "Well… you could look worse, I suppose."

When I grin, she's sinks to her knees by the couch, then wraps me up in a warm, gentle hug.

"I can't believe this happened to you," she whispers, and I can hear the emotion in her voice. "If you had died on me, I swear I'd never forgive you."

"I'd never do that to you," I whisper back, tightening the embrace.

When she pulls back, she peers closer at my temple. "That bastard. Have they found him?"

I shake my head. Just that small movement hurts. They gave me some pain medicine at the hospital, but I haven't taken it yet. I'm okay with good old-fashioned Tylenol to take the edge off, but the edge still has a bit of a bite. I was told I'd feel better in a few days, though.

I'd already told Jorie all the details yesterday when I called her after I got home. I waited until then so she wouldn't rush off to the hospital. When it was late enough, I could feign being too tired to have her visit. I knew she'd want to come, but she hadn't needed to. I was going to be fine.

Physically, for sure.

Emotionally might be another thing. I've found myself a little weepy this morning, and I can't figure out why. I'm naturally a strong woman. The one who steps up in a crisis. Remains calm and collected. I'm the bearer of responsibility. The one who cares for people.

And yet... the slightest thing makes me want to cry today.

My mom fluttering all around me.

Luis being overly solicitous when he stopped by twice today to check on me.

My dad taking an earlier flight back just to assure himself his only girl was okay.

Jorie alternating between wanting to organize a man hunt for my assailant to wanting to break down into a puddle of tears on my behalf.

And Benjamin... I want to cry because he's been very, very silent since he left the hospital yesterday.

I'm no fool. I could tell he was off-kilter the moment our eyes locked in the emergency room. He was beyond bothered over what happened to me. I could sense the anger, frustration, and fear within him. The way he'd coolly assessed my medical condition without giving me what I needed—emotional support—really hurt. I could tell how bothered he was when I recounted my story, and then... it had hurt again when he couldn't get out of there quick enough.

Sure, I let him lay it all on his job and the need to get back to his patients, but we both know he could have stayed if he wanted.

He just didn't want to, and, yes, that's what's making me feel so sad most of all.

Jorie looks over her shoulder into the kitchen where my mom is making some chicken tortilla soup for me. It's my favorite.

She then raises an eyebrow at me. "Where the fuck is Benjamin?"

Leave it to Jorie to be able to know exactly what's bothering me the most.

I shrug. "He picked up an unexpected on-call shift this morning."

At least that's what he told me—via text. When he'd left the hospital last night, he'd given me a kiss on my lips and whispered, "I'll try to come see you tomorrow depending on work."

I knew it was a lie then.

It had been confirmed this morning when I'd gotten his text.

Granted, his text then went on to ask a bunch of questions about how I was feeling. Clinical, flat, unemotional questions.

I didn't bother answering them other than to say I felt fine and not to worry about me.

That was over four hours ago, and I haven't heard anything else from him. I get our relationship is new, but the way things have been going these past few weeks— particularly after our talk on the boat on the Fourth of July—I expected more of him.

And I'm not stupid either. I know what's going on.

It's not that Benjamin doesn't have it within him to

be supportive and caring in a situation like this. I know he does.

It's that this entire situation has freaked him out and catapulted him backward, straight into the fear-based way he'd been living.

"I think it's over between Benjamin and me," I murmur, expressing the fear I've been analyzing all morning. The tears once again prick at my eyes.

Jorie pushes up, moves her ass onto the side of the couch near my hip, and gives me a concerned glance. "What makes you say that?"

"Because he's not here," I mutter almost petulantly.

"But you said he's on call," she replies with a frown.

I sigh, knowing I'm not making sense. "Yeah... I know. He's on call. But I think he took it on purpose to avoid me."

"Okay, slow down... back up. Start from the beginning and tell me what's going on, because just the day before yesterday when we talked, everything was going fabulously. You even told me you were fairly sure you were falling in love with him."

That's true. I'd confided that to my best friend, which meant it was true. I wouldn't have said it otherwise, and I still feel that way. It's why it hurts so bad he's not here right now, or at least doing a bit better job of checking in on me.

I've never really told Jorie anything Benjamin discussed with me about the way he lived the past year. I think she's surmised some of it, but the things Benjamin has told me directly I've held close between us and won't share.

But I do my best to describe the hurdles we've had to overcome. "Benjamin, as you can imagine, had sort of shut himself off from the world after the accident."

Jorie nods. She knows this.

"It was not only his way of burying the pain of his losses, but also ensuring it doesn't happen again."

"Don't ever care for someone, then you'll never be hurt when that person is taken away," she summarizes.

"Exactly," I say. "And well… Benjamin and I have developed feelings for each other. He's risked his heart to open up, and I think what happened to me might have been a very stark reminder of why he had kept himself closed off in the first place."

"You think he's dumping you because this was what? Too scary for him?" she asks with an incredulous expression on her face.

"He hasn't actually dumped me," I say with a trace of bitterness in my voice. "But it's coming. I know it. Even when he came to the hospital to see me yesterday, I felt him pull away. I could see the disconnect in his eyes."

"It doesn't make sense," she mutters.

"It does if you understand he cares too much for me. Yesterday was a stark reminder of the frailty of life, and he doesn't want that pain again."

Jorie grimaces. "You sound so understanding and

accepting. I'm pissed at him."

"You don't love him," I point out. "I do under-stand."

"But it hurts, right?" she asks tentatively.

"Hurts like fuck," I admit.

"What are you going to do?" she asks, knowing me well enough to know I'll never sit back and wonder about these things.

"Can you drive me to Vegas?"

She blinks in surprise. "Right now?"

"Now," I affirm with a solid nod of my head, which hurts like hell. I push up on the couch, dislodging Jorie from my side. She stands, then holds a hand out to me, so I latch on. She hauls me up, and I grimace from the lance of pain through my head.

I can see she wants to push me back down to make me rest, but she also knows I won't rest until I figure out what Benjamin's thinking and whether we are, in fact, over.

If he can't handle this, then I'll gracefully back away. I don't want to cause him more pain. He's been through his lifetime's share already. I also don't want things to drag out between us. I don't want drama.

One of the reasons Benjamin and I have meshed so well is because we are both transparent with our wants and needs.

I need him to tell me the truth. If he's even half the man I think he is, I know he'll give it to me straight.

CHAPTER 29

Benjamin

THE ON-CALL ROOM is blessedly empty, and I sit on one of the couches to take a moment to try to decompress. I haven't had a surgery yet, but I'd been called in on a few consults I'm continuing to monitor. A ruptured blood vessel in the brain, which we're attempting to treat with medication at this point. It might require a ventriculostomy if the swelling doesn't decrease. The other was a spinal injury from a fall off a ladder, which caused a ruptured disc that's compressing on the spinal column. Again, treating conservatively for now, but it could turn into a surgery at any time.

No high-pressure situations yet, so that's why I need to decompress.

That all has to do with Elena because outside the blissful moments where I must concentrate on my patients or their test results, my mind has been occupied with her. I'm incredibly worried about her still. While I know she's physically fine, I'm more worried about the mental toll she's suffering. I know what it's like to confront death. It can fuck with people's head.

I really should give her a call and check in.

I don't, though, because I don't know what to say. Every fiber in my being is still saying I should pull away. Get out while I'm still able to do so with only a slightly broken heart versus a crushed one later down the line. If I'm going to break things off with her, that needs to be done face to face and not over the phone.

And yet, by not calling her or even texting to ask how she's doing today, I'm sending a clear message she's not important to me.

Which is about as far from the truth as possible.

She's too fucking important is the problem, and I should have known this was coming. When I'd broken things off with her before Father's Day because I'd realized she made me vulnerable, I should have left her far behind and moved on.

I snag my phone out of my lab coat, then check to see if she's sent any messages.

I'm both relieved and sad there aren't any, because I wouldn't have minded her alleviating my worry with a quick update.

Regardless, I do need to check on one thing, so I dial my mother. I roll my eyes at the way she answers. "Hi, Benji. How's your day going?"

Benji was what she called me when I was little, and that's never stopped. She doesn't call me that all the time, but usually when she's feeling overly affectionate. She's been saying it a lot lately since we reconnected, and I give it to her. It's the least I can do after the hurt I've caused her the past year.

"Just checking in… making sure everything is good for tomorrow," I say. She's flying in for a short visit. I'm really looking forward to it, now more than ever.

"I'm already packed. Assuming nothing happens with a flight delay, I will see you tomorrow morning."

"Awesome," I say. "I've got the day off, so we'll go do something fun."

"Can Elena come?" she asks, because of course I told my mom all about her. Stupid me thought it was an appropriate time to divulge, share something important with my mom so she knows I'm ready for all the ways we used to be close.

"Um… I'm actually not sure that's going to happen," I say lamely.

"Why?" she exclaims, sounding incredibly disappointed.

I tell her what happened to Elena yesterday. And then I explain how I feel about it. "It scared the shit out of me, Mom. And it made me think… I'm just not ready for this. Ready to put myself out there like that with someone again. I mean, maybe in the future, but right now… I just don't think I can handle it."

She's silent a moment before finally saying, "You can handle only what you can handle, Benjamin. Either way,

I've got your back. I'll pray God gives you the strength to work through it."

"Really, Mom?" I ask angrily. "You're going to bring *him* into it?"

"You may not have a relationship with Him, but I do, so yes... I'll pray."

Why the fuck does everyone love this guy so much? "God doesn't have shit to do with my life."

"Of course He does," she replies firmly, not to dismiss my beliefs—or rather the lack thereof—but to solidly remind me that her faith is strong.

"Then why in the hell didn't he stop April and Cassidy from dying?"

"It's not His job to prevent bad things, Benjamin," she says quietly. "But rather to give you the strength to get through it."

"But he didn't," I mutter.

"I believe He did," she replies gently.

"Elena believes in God," I say. Why I say that, I don't know. "She told me yesterday God must have been looking out for her. That it was why she made it out alive. And if that's the case, then why was he looking out for Elena, but not April and Cassidy?"

"Benji... honey," my mom drawls soothingly. "We'll never know for sure. Maybe God wasn't looking out for Elena, but rather the gunman."

"What?" I rasp, my throat tightening with surprise at her suggestion.

"Maybe God had another purpose for that man or didn't want him to have the weight of killing someone. Maybe God brought April and Cassidy home where they were meant to be because maybe you're meant to be with Elena. We just never know. We can't know. All we can do is have faith He ultimately wants what's best for us, and he will give us nothing more than what we can handle."

I'm so tired of this circular argument with people. I know Elena would love to be involved in this right now, as her beliefs align very closely with my mom's. But none of her words make me feel better. They don't bring clarity.

They only confuse and exhaust me.

"Look... I've got to get going," I say. "But I'll be at the airport to get you tomorrow, okay?"

"Okay, honey. I love you."

"Love you too," I murmur before disconnecting the phone.

I push up from the couch, then walk over to one of the vending machines. Nothing looks good. I move back to the couch.

Before I can sit down, my phone chimes with a text from Elena. I look down at it. *I'm here in the lobby. I know you're on call, but I'd love if you can spare me a few minutes. I'll wait for however long I need to.*

Shit... she's here. I'm both elated and terrified. While I had every intention of us talking—breaking up, maybe—I hadn't expected it to be today. But that's my Elena... forcing a showdown because she's not one to sit back and wait to see how life works out.

On my way, I text back, then snag my cane from near the doorway.

It takes me several minutes to make my way to her, mainly due to overcrowded elevators.

She doesn't see me coming, and it affords me the ability to look her over critically. I see the bruising and stitches. I'd expected them, so it wasn't a shocker.

What I hate seeing is the misery on her face. She knows.

She knows I'm a bastard and ready to bolt. Without her saying a word, I can read every beautiful nuance on her. It's obvious she's going to let me do it, too.

I'm within half-a-dozen paces from her when she sees me and our eyes lock. She doesn't move toward me, and I come to a stop a few feet from her. "How are you feeling? Headaches? Any dizziness? Double vision?"

Annoyance flashes in her eyes, and she pointedly ignores my questions. "I need to know if we're over."

A rush of air pushes out of my lungs as I glance around the immediate vicinity for somewhere private to talk. Too many damn people.

I take Elena's hand in mine, then lead her out the lobby doors and around the side of the hospital where there's an outdoor courtyard. There are a few people here, but I find a quiet bench under a tree.

SAWYER BENNETT

We sit, angling in toward each other, her knees brushing against mine. I reach out, then brush a lock of hair back from her forehead on the opposite side of her wound. She watches me carefully as if reading something into my action. I just wanted to be able to see her entire face.

"I wasn't completely honest with you in the past," I begin, and she blinks in surprise. "About when I stood you up for our date at The Wicked Horse just before Father's Day."

"You were feeling overwhelmed," she says, but I shake my head.

"It was far beyond overwhelmed, Elena." I reach out, take her hand. "You completely stripped away all of my defenses. Laid me bare and think back to then... that's before we really started opening up about our feelings. That early on, you scared the shit out of me because you made me vulnerable again."

"I'm sorry," she mumbles, looking away for a moment before coming back to me. "I don't even know what to say to that."

"Don't apologize," I chide. "I'm telling you only so you'll know how powerfully you affected me, even back then. You opened me up in ways I didn't think possible, nor did I think I was ready for it. So I panicked and totally ghosted you."

"That's all well and good," she replies, stroking a thumb over the back of my hand. "That gives me better insight, but you let me back in, even knowing the risk."

"I did, because you also made me start forgetting the pain," I admit, and I can see realization set in. "Here I am, falling for this beautiful, smart, and vivacious woman, and my life was starting to get really good again. Until—"

"Until I just reminded you how fragile it all is," she says softly, and I can tell this also isn't news. She'd already figured this all out because her tone is defeated and accepting all at once. "You don't want to risk that type of loss again."

"I don't know, Elena," I say truthfully. "Every instinct says run, but I don't know if I can let you go. Regardless, all of it is a testament to how much I've come to care for you. I wish I didn't. It would make things so much easier if I could just go back to loving to fuck you rather than just lo—"

I stop before I admit the "L" word out loud.

"I feel like I should say something to sway you my way," she says. "Get mad. Goad you or something. But I can't force you to make me important enough to risk the pain, and that's really what it boils down to."

I take her other hand, hold both tightly. "You're important, Elena. So fucking important. Too important. And I'm not trying to compare you to April because you're both so different and wonderful in your own rights. I mean, neither of you could ever measure up to the other because you're both so unique, yet... I find myself comparing the pain I felt to the potential pain I could bear with you, and Elena… I think if I lost you, it would destroy me."

She shakes her head, a sad smile on her face. "No, you would be fine eventually. You would survive and move on, and I know that because I believe in you."

And then she stands, pulling her hands from mine. "Goodbye, Benjamin."

I'm stunned, and I scramble to stand as well, grabbing my cane and punching it onto the brick walkway. "That's it? You're leaving? You're not even going to try to tell me I'm wrong?"

She tilts her head, giving me an admonishing smile. "I just did. Told you that you're wrong. You'd survive because you're strong. I personally think you have the fortitude to move past these fears, and I'm hoping you'll prove me right. You know where to find me if that's the case."

She then moves past me, her arm brushing against my chest. My hand snakes out, fingers intertwining with hers for just a moment. Neither of us looks at one another, but we linger in that touch until she pulls her hand free and walks away from me.

CHAPTER 30

Elena

I DON'T AGREE with some of the Catholic church's doctrines, but I don't think that matters. I think it's good to question and make decisions for myself. Even though I don't see eye to eye with my church on all things, I find immense comfort within these brick walls.

The smell of incense, the stained-glass windows representing the Stations of the Cross, the ceremony of Communion. All of it gives me comfort, starting my week off right.

My entire family attends each week, although one of us might skip for a good reason here and there—and yes, I realize spending the day in bed with a man is not a good enough reason. After church, we'll often go out to an early lunch together, a favorite being Olive Garden.

Today, everyone is in attendance, which in addition to my parents includes five brothers, three sisters-in-law, two nephews, and four nieces, although the newest little niece, Emily, is in the cry room with her mom this morning. We take up two pews, the Costieri family, but such is the Catholic way of life. It feels good to be out and about, especially after I hugged my parents' couch most of yesterday.

I had been slightly annoyed at the way my mom had hovered over me all morning, but by the time Jorie had brought me back from my breakup with Benjamin, all I'd wanted was my mom to baby me.

I mean… I think we broke up. I try to replay our last words, and I'm not sure. We'd left it sort of vague. Benjamin said he feared the pain of losing me, I'd said he was stronger than he gave himself credit for, and then… I walked away. That part felt right for sure. I'd said all I could.

Communion has just concluded, the last few rows of parishioners filing back into place. Our priest is making some announcements, and I've tuned out. I slip my phone out of my purse, which was put on vibrate the minute I walked in after an incredibly embarrassing moment about two years ago when "Hell's Bells" rang out loudly one time when my boyfriend called me.

I shoot off a quick text to Jorie. *Let's go shopping for baby clothes today.*

Ever at the ready to have my back. *Sure you wouldn't rather go to a bar and just get drunk?*

You're pregnant. You can't drink.

But I can listen, she wrote back. *And be your DD.*

My mother leans over to hiss in my ear. "You put

that phone away right now, young lady. We are in God's house."

Smirking, I duck my head and shoot Jorie a quick text. *Call you in a few minutes once I get out of church.*

Tilting my head up, I find my mom glaring at me, but she can't hide the tiny quirk to her lips because part of her likes I'm still a brat. Her eyes move to my stitches and soften, mouth turning into a frown. She knows not only my head was broken, but also my heart was as well. She gives me a pat on my leg before returning her attention up to the altar. The ending processional has started, and the congregation stands.

I sing under my breath as I have the worst voice in the world. After the processional, we start to file out of the pews. I follow my mom, nodding and smiling at people I know. We shuffle down the main aisle, the process slow-going as people will be pausing to shake hands and say a few words with our priest at the doors.

Keeping my head down so as not to run over my mom, I consider Jorie's proposal. Maybe getting drunk today isn't such a bad idea. It could temporarily obliterate Benjamin from my mind. Or it could make me stupid enough to drunk call him.

Ugh. Not a good idea.

And then, for some reason, I know I must look up. I raise my head, scanning the back pews, and right there… in the last row on the end, Benjamin sits and stares.

He's dressed in a tan suit with a pale blue shirt. Hair

slicked back rather than his mussed look, beard perfectly trimmed.

Benjamin.

Sitting in an actual house of God. I'm surprised he hasn't burst into flames over the abhorrence I'm sure he's feeling to be in here.

When he smiles, my heart trips. He gives a slight jerk of his head toward the exit, a silent request I meet him outside. I nod in return.

Standing with cane in hand, he merges into the shuffling crowd ahead of me and I lose sight of him.

Eager to see what he's doing here, I give a tiny nudge to my mom's back, urging her to move faster. Of course she can't, and she whips around to glare. I duck my head, giving her a submissive apology.

Practically bouncing from foot to foot as we make our way out of church, a million thoughts run through my head.

He's here to proclaim his love.

Or give me a pair of panties I'd mistakenly left at his place.

No, he wouldn't come to church to do that.

Would he?

I mean... maybe to thumb his nose at God?

Ugh... why can't these people hurry?

And then, my parents are shaking hands with the priest. I'm almost free. I resist the urge to push them past Father Gaul, then I'm right in front of him. His kind blue eyes rest on my stitches, and he brings his hand to the top of my head.

He murmurs a short prayer, then says, "I've been praying for you, my child."

"Thank you, Father Gaul," I say softly, then turn away from him, but my mother blocks my way.

Going to my tiptoes, I scan the crowd below the dozen or so steps leading out of the church. I can't see Benjamin anywhere.

Maybe he was a figment of my imagination. Or someone who looked like Benjamin.

The people in the crowd are moving a little more freely, crisscrossing my line of sight and moving left and right to the two parking lots on either side of the church.

And then… like God parting the Red Sea for Moses, a path parts and I finally see him.

Across the street, leaning against his Audi that's parked there.

It's a damn *Sixteen Candles* moment. He's even got his hands tucked into his pocket, pulling one out to hesitantly wave.

I resist the dorky move to look around as if it's not me he's here for, because I know better than that. Putting my hand on my mom's shoulder, I lean into her. "I'm going to skip lunch today."

She turns to me. "Are you feeling okay?"

I nod toward Benjamin. "Yes."

Her eyes slide across the street to take him in. She's

my mom, so her lips flatten and she glares at him before saying, "His apology better be good."

"Might not be an apology at all," I say.

"If that's the case, call me and I'll set your brothers on him. They'll teach him a lesson."

I snort, then lean in to give her a kiss. "Call you later, Mamá. Love you."

"Love you too," she replies.

Taking a deep breath, I stare at Benjamin. He doesn't move to me, but rather waves me over to him. I note he doesn't have his cane now so he must have put it in the car, which must mean he doesn't plan on staying long.

Oh shit… this is probably a final breakup meeting.

My stomach turns with dread as I make my way down the steps. I stop for several cars before I'm able to cross the street.

Smiling, he pushes off the Audi.

"What are you doing here?" I ask.

"There's someone I want you to meet," he replies. I'm dumbfounded, thinking this is beyond weird.

Benjamin takes my hand and leads me around the back of his car to the passenger side. The front window rolls down and I stare at a woman who, while I've never seen a picture of her, I know she's Benjamin's mom. She was flying in this morning for a visit, which is something I'd managed to put out of my mind until just now.

I smooth my hair down in a nervous gesture. Benjamin's hand goes to my lower back, urging me forward just a bit closer as if assuring me she won't bite. His mom smiles broadly, then sticks a hand out the window. "Hi, Elena... it's so wonderful to meet you."

Of course, I take her hand, but my smile falters. I'm faltering. "Nice to meet you, too, Mrs. Hewitt."

She waves a hand. "Please... call me Kathy."

Not able to contain my confusion anymore, I just ask Benjamin point blank, "What's going on here?"

His mother smiles before the window slowly rolls up to give us privacy. Benjamin looks a little discombobulated as he glances over the top of his car back to the church.

"That was weird," he says softly, giving a nod at the chapel. "Sitting in church."

"Not your thing," I remind him. "I get it."

"It could be my thing," he replies, eyes on me. "With you, that is."

I shake my head, brows furrowed. "I'm sorry... I feel like I'm in the twilight zone. Yesterday, I got the distinct impression we were over, and now you show up at my church with your mom."

Benjamin chuckles as he points a finger at the passenger window behind which his mother sits. "That's sort of my grand gesture."

I frown in further confusion. "Grand gesture?"

He gives me a sheepish smile and a tiny shrug. "I thought introducing you to my mother would show you how serious I am."

"Serious about what?" I ask, although I'm starting to clue in at this point.

"About you," he replies, hand going to tuck a lock of hair behind my ear. His eyes roam over my face. "I wanted to show you I wasn't afraid to move forward. To build on what we already have. Make a life together."

My head swims from the implications of those words. He seems so sure, yet... he's flaked out on me because of his fears twice now.

"That's a big turnaround from yesterday," I say.

He shakes his head. "Not really. I knew what my choices were, and I just had to make the decision. Go forward or backward. It was pretty simple once I really thought about it."

"Simple?" I ask with a wry smile.

"Yeah," he replies, his hands coming to my waist to draw me closer. My hands rest on his arms, and I tip my head back to look up at him. "My love for you simply outweighed my fears."

"Love?" My voice is so faint I can barely hear it, but, fortunately, he does.

He nods, his eyes solemnly locked onto mine. "Yeah... I love you, Elena. So incredibly deeply. I can't let you just walk out of my life. In fact, I've been thinking, and I'm fairly sure God put you in my path for a reason."

"What's that?" I whisper.

"So I can live again," he says. "Love again. It's a gift that's been handed to me, and I can't ignore it. So please put me out of my misery and tell me I still have a chance with you. I haven't irrevocably ruined things, right?"

My smile is coy as I shake my head, stepping in closer. I bring my hands up to touch the nape of his neck, then go to my tiptoes to put my face as close to his as I can. "I love you, too."

"Thank fuck," he mutters just before kissing me. A sweet, soul-stealing kiss that's filled with so much promise my heart flutters in response.

He pulls back. "I'm in it for good, Elena. I promise."

I give him my own pledge in return. "I'm right there with you. Always."

Benjamin grins, rubbing his nose alongside mine. When I have his eyes again, he nods at the car. "Ideally, I'd love to whisk you back to your place or mine to seal this all with orgasms, but I got Mom along for the ride. I was thinking of treating you ladies to a five-star lunch. Can you break plans with your family today?"

"They'll totally understand," I say, making a note to text Jorie as soon as I get into the car.

"Then your chariot awaits," he says as he opens the back door with a flourish.

"I can get in the backseat," Kathy immediately says, but I'm already sliding in.

"No way," I say as I reach for the seat belt. "I'm good back here."

Benjamin watches me for just a moment, making sure my legs are in. He mouths the words to me again.

I love you.

I silently give them back. As he shuts the door, the last thing I see is a satisfied grin on his face.

Kathy turns in her seat. "Okay... start talking. Tell me all about yourself."

We're chatting away like old friends by the time Benjamin rounds the car and gets into the driver's side to whisk us off to lunch. He doesn't interrupt or say a word, just drives with that same satisfied smile on his face.

EPILOGUE

Elena

I FORCE THE last bite of steak in my mouth because I'm so stuffed I don't think I can manage this last bite, but it's so damn good I must. I chew slowly, savoring the flavor. Benjamin spared no expense on celebrating our four-month anniversary, and it's beyond ridiculously cute he wants to celebrate it. He brought me to CUT by Wolfgang Puck, and my eyes bugged out of my head at the prices. It's been a bit of an adjustment accepting I'm dating someone who thinks nothing of feeding me a sixty-five-dollar bone-in filet while he dines on the one-hundred-and-thirty-dollar porterhouse.

"They have the most amazing chocolate torte for dessert here," he says as he watches me swallow my last bite of food, forearms crossed on the table.

"I can't," I say as I wipe my mouth, placing my napkin back on my lap. "I'll actually explode if I eat another bite of food, and that would be very ugly. Totally ruin the mood for what I have planned for you later this evening."

"And what's that?" he asks with great interest, leaning forward just a bit.

I wag my finger at him. "It's a surprise, but I promise you'll be barking like a dog when I'm done with you."

Benjamin wrinkles his nose. "Not sure I'm all that interested now."

"Screaming my name out to the neighbors?" I suggest instead.

"Now that has merit," he replies with a laugh as he pushes up from the table. "Excuse me a moment, though… I'll be right back."

"Take your time, babe," I reply. I watch him only a moment as he walks away. His limp is still there, but he's been going out more and more without his cane. He's been working on strengthening his leg at the gym, and he's suffering less pain with weight bearing.

Not that it matters to me. He's sexy with or without the cane—limp or no limp.

While Benjamin's gone, I continue to sip at my red wine and surf my phone. I shoot a quick text to Jorie to check in on her. Her pregnancy is going smoothly, and she looks so utterly adorable with her baby bump that I can't stop buying cute, tight dresses for her that showcase my new goddaughter who will be arriving in a few months' time.

"Well, don't you look ravishing tonight?" a male voice says from across the table. It sounds vaguely familiar. After my head pops up, I blink in surprise at August Greenfield sitting across from me. I haven't seen him since the night in the Wicked Horse when I'd almost had a threesome with him and Cage.

Of course, Benjamin and I rarely go to the Wicked Horse. He gave up his membership. If we're feeling especially frisky, he'll pay the onetime fee and I'll use the special membership Jorie got me. But we've been maybe three times since he introduced me to his mom and things changed for the better.

August sits in Benjamin's chair, giving me a wickedly handsome grin, both dimples popping. I just cock an eyebrow, wondering what his game is.

"This is where you say back to me, 'Gee, August… you look mighty fine yourself'." His eyes sparkle with mischief.

"You're all right," I say with a smirk, crossing my arms over my chest. "Funny how you waited until Benjamin was gone before you came to say hello."

"Well, my interest isn't in Benjamin," he drawls.

"Well," I reply tartly. "It better not be in me, because my only interest is in Benjamin."

August crosses his hands over his heart, jerking like I'd just shot an arrow there. "Ouch, that hurts."

I snort. "No, it doesn't."

"I thought we really had a connection, Elena," he says with a pout.

"Your face is going to have a connection with my fist

if you don't get out of my chair," Benjamin says as he comes up behind August. But he doesn't say it with any real menace. It's almost an idle promise.

Smirking, I nod toward Benjamin. "I'd do what he says. He's also a hair puller."

August throws his head back and laughs, easily vacating Benjamin's chair. To my surprise, he thrusts his hand at Benjamin, who hesitantly takes it.

He glances between Benjamin and me as he shakes his hand. "Actually... I saw the two of you over here having dinner, so I just wanted to come over to congratulate you. That night in the Wicked Horse, I sort of figured Elena had gone permanently off the market."

Benjamin growls low, and August rushes to clarify, "I didn't mean off the "meat" market so to speak. I meant as far as relationships go."

Benjamin rolls his eyes, unbuttons his suit jacket to sit in his chair, and pointedly ignores August.

I give him a sweet smile. "Well, it's nice seeing you again, but—"

August holds his hands up in surrender, a deep laugh following it. "I get it... I'm intruding."

"Yes, you are," Benjamin mutters.

"Best of luck to both of you," August says. With an evil glint in his eyes, he murmurs right to me, "But if you ever dump this guy, Elena... you know where to find me."

Benjamin growls again. August snorts before retreating quickly. I pick my napkin up to pretend to wipe my mouth again, but really, I'm stifling a laugh.

"Funny guy," Benjamin mutters as he watches me, a slight lift to one corner of his mouth.

"Men are so weird… the little games you play. People think women are the only ones who do that stuff, but men are just as bad."

A waiter approaches, a white plate in hand, and sits a chocolate torte down in front of me. I'm so full I can't even look at the damn thing.

I shake my head, my gaze going across the table. "I told you I'm stuffed."

The waiter brandishes two spoons, sitting one beside the plate and handing another to a grinning Benjamin. "I think I can manage to eat enough of this for the both of us."

"Have at it," I say with a laugh.

We chat, and I sip my wine. Benjamin takes small bites of the torte, reaching across the table each time rather than just pulling the plate his way. Every other bite or so, he remarks how good it is and that I should try some.

I merely shake my head to decline each time.

Finally, he gives me a look of mild annoyance. "You're not making this easy."

"Making what easy?" I ask.

"Can you at least look at the plate?"

"Huh?" I say with a frown, then dip my head to see

what he's talking about.

On the plate is a demolished torte, one lonely bite left behind with some crumbs. What I had failed to notice when the plate was set down was there was elegant cursive writing in chocolate around the edge of the white china.

Will you marry me?

I snap my head up to look at Benjamin, mouth dropping open. He's smiling, holding up a black velvet box.

He opens it, and my mouth drops open even wider as I take in the massive teardrop-shaped diamond twinkling so fiercely in the candlelight I'm almost blinded.

"Oh my God," I murmur, one hand fluttering to the base of my throat.

"I thought we agreed God doesn't have a direct hand in playing with our lives like this," Benjamin chides. He and I have had deep discussions about God, divinity, and what His purpose in our lives is. He even goes to church with me most Sundays, though he sometimes likes to just be lazy and stay home, which is okay, too.

My heart swells at his pointed reminder our God is very mysterious in his ways, and that the ring glistening in front of me only has to do with the man holding the box.

Because he loves me and wants to marry me.

The realization is shocking. I mean, we'd grown so close over the last few months. We've integrated our lives permanently as he bought a home about halfway in between Vegas and Henderson. We moved in together quickly, and we've been sharing our dreams for the future together.

But we'd never outright discussed marriage, so this is an incredible surprise to me.

"Elena," he says, and I drag my gaze from the diamond to him. "No one ever starts out their adult lives thinking they'll be married twice. But I've learned our lives may have phases, which can include more than one type of love. You know how I feel about April and Cassidy. You've patiently listened to me talk about them over these past months. You've given me a safe environment to do so, always encouraging me to never forget what I had with them."

This is true. I'd even demanded Benjamin pull his photos of them out and place them around our house, so he never forgets or diminishes their memories again.

"But while I'll always cherish them, they are my past and you are my future. It's going to be a long, beautiful future together. One I hope is filled with children, and, one day, grandchildren. I want to grow old with you. Share all of life's grand adventures with you. I love you more than anything in this world or beyond, and I'm begging you to please make me the happiest man alive by agreeing to marry me."

It's at this point I have tears flowing freely down my face, and snot threatens to drip from my nose. I take my napkin, hastily dabbing the offending wetness away before I'm able to give him an enthusiastic nod of assent.

Relief floods his face, and he rises out of his chair. I stand, meeting him at the side of the table. Then my left hand is in his, and he's sliding the ring onto my finger. It's dazzling, and I'm mesmerized by how big it is. I've never seen anything like it.

"I love you," Benjamin murmurs as he brings my hand up, brushing a kiss on my knuckles.

"Oh, Benjamin... I love you, too," I say, throwing my arms around him so I can bestow the biggest, sloppiest, most emotional kiss in the world on him. His arms go tightly around me, and he lifts me off the ground as our kiss deepens.

I'm vaguely aware of people clapping, and I'm acutely aware I've never been this happy in my entire life.

The best thing, though, is it's only going to get better from here.

Wicked Secret is coming May 26, 2020!
Reserve your copy now!

Want more Wicked Horse Vegas? GO HERE to see all
of the sinfully sexy standalones available in the Wicked
Horse Vegas series.

sawyerbennett.com/bookstore/the-wicked-horse-vegas-series

Connect with Sawyer online:

Website: sawyerbennett.com

Twitter: twitter.com/bennettbooks

Facebook: facebook.com/bennettbooks

Instagram: instagram.com/sawyerbennett123

Book+Main Bites:

bookandmainbites.com/sawyerbennett

Goodreads: goodreads.com/Sawyer_Bennett

Amazon: amazon.com/author/sawyerbennett

BookBub: bookbub.com/authors/sawyer-bennett

About the Author

Since the release of her debut contemporary romance novel, Off Sides, in January 2013, Sawyer Bennett has released multiple books, many of which have appeared on the New York Times, USA Today and Wall Street Journal bestseller lists.

A reformed trial lawyer from North Carolina, Sawyer uses real life experience to create relatable, sexy stories that appeal to a wide array of readers. From new adult to erotic contemporary romance, Sawyer writes something for just about everyone.

Sawyer likes her Bloody Marys strong, her martinis dirty, and her heroes a combination of the two. When not bringing fictional romance to life, Sawyer is a chauffeur, stylist, chef, maid, and personal assistant to a very active daughter, as well as full-time servant to her adorably naughty dogs. She believes in the good of others, and that a bad day can be cured with a great work-out, cake, or even better, both.

Sawyer also writes general and women's fiction under the pen name S. Bennett and sweet romance under the name Juliette Poe.

Made in the USA
Middletown, DE
20 April 2020